FOREVER AT RISK

TERROR, MN SERIES

LARISSA EMERALD

Forever at Risk
Terror, MN Series – Novel

Copyright © 2018 Castle Oak Publishing LLC

ISBN-13: 978-1-942139-19-5

http://www.larissaemerald.com

Published in the United States of America.

BOOKS BY LARISSA EMERALD

Paranormal Romance

DIVINE TREE GUARDIAN SERIES
Awakening Fire
Awakening Touch
Awakening Storm

VAMPIRE
Forever at Dawn
Forever at Midnight

TERROR, MN PARANORMAL
Forever at Risk
Forever Found

PARANORMAL THRILLER
Perfection

NOCTURNE FALLS UNIVERSE
The Vampire Bounty Hunter's Unexpected Catch
The Shaman Charms the Shifter
Merry & Bright Anthology – The Witch's Snow Globe
Wish
The Dragon Falls for the Fairy Godmother

ROMANTIC SUSPENSE
Winter Heat

CONTEMPORARY ROMANCE
Come Sail Away – Barefoot Bay Novella

THE STORY

Founded by angels, harassed by demons, the town of Terror, MN is hidden in the northern Minnesota countryside. Obey the rules and it's a fun town. #1 rule: Do NOT eat thy neighbor.

The sheriff of Terror, dragon shifter Val Solberg has kept a vampire criminal under wraps for almost a year. But now the culprit's fans are creating havoc among the local vampires. Val turns to the one person he doesn't want help from, his ex, sorceress Twyla McGuire. He'd allowed his job to come between them before. He didn't think he could deny her again. Will he save the town and lose his heart?

Loving Val has never been a problem. It's forgiving him that seems impossible. Now she must decide to risk giving him a second chance, or let him go for good.

TERROR, MINNESOTA

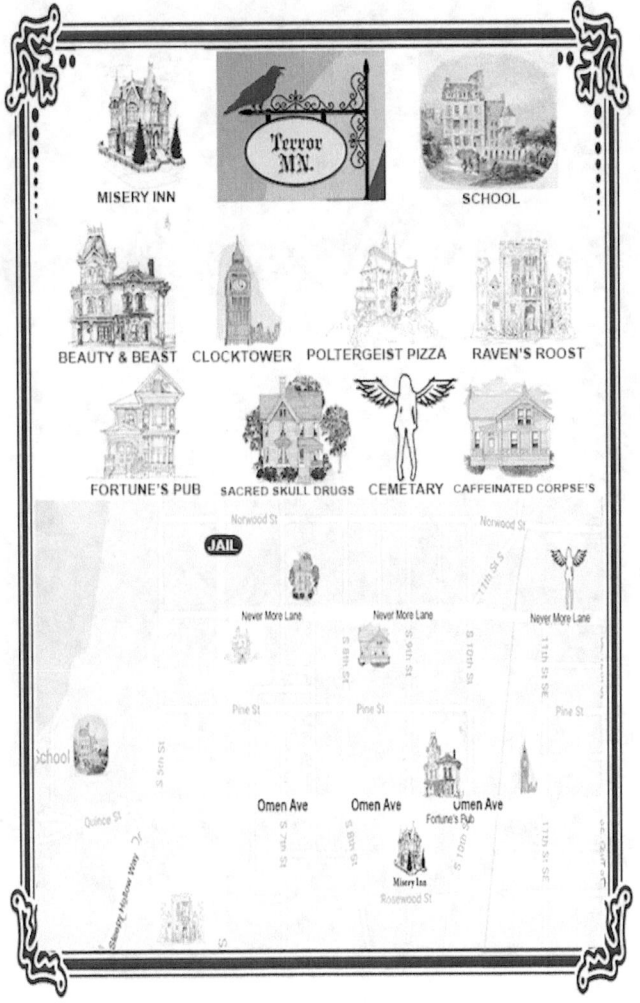

MISERY INN

Terror MN.

SCHOOL

BEAUTY & BEAST   CLOCKTOWER   POLTERGEIST PIZZA   RAVEN'S ROOST

FORTUNE'S PUB   SACRED SKULL DRUGS   CEMETARY   CAFFEINATED CORPSE'S

Norwood St   Norwood St

JAIL

Never More Lane   Never More Lane   Never More Lane

Pine St   Pine St   Pine St

School

Omen Ave   Omen Ave   Omen Ave
Fortune's Pub

Quince St

Misery Inn
Rosewood St

Forever at Risk

Sheriff Val Solberg moved deeper into the coal-black alley. Pausing, he angled his head and listened. The sounds of insects in the night bounced off the buildings while water trickled into the gutter. He heard no slap of footsteps or heavy breathing to indicate anyone in the Council had been followed.

Good. Responsible for the safety of Terror, MN, and charged with keeping law and order in the town, Val was the only nonvoting *guest* who attended the secret Paranormal Council meetings. His job entailed making sure the Council remained clandestine while carrying out their decrees.

In a town filled with paranormal beings, holding a meeting was damn difficult. Most supernaturals had extremely heightened senses. They could track creatures without much effort. Fortunately, elder witch Nora McGuire was the head of the Paranormal Council in Terror. She had the power to cast a spell over the meetings, a glamour making them nearly impossible to detect. Still, he couldn't count on that entirely. They'd had an uprising in the veakling vampire community of late ever since one of their leaders had been thrown in jail. The vampire race had been diluted over the years, and veaklings were at the bottom of the gene pool. At the top were the original ancestors, who had traveled from the planet Cest and had extremely pure bloodlines. But veaklings were driven by baser needs and a lust for drinking blood from innocent victims. Val's stomach churned with a shiver of disgust.

Such was the likes of his prisoner Payton Grey. In his opinion, they needed to be done with him.

Sometimes, the group met in the committee persons' homes. More frequently, however, the meetings occurred in a neutral, revolving location. Tonight, they gathered in the basement beneath the town's clock tower.

Satisfied their rendezvous would be safe, Val hurried to the back of the alley. He ducked into the previously selected doorway, then locked the solid wooden door behind him. After lumbering down the stone stairs, he entered the dimly lit basement where the eight committee members were seated at a long cherry-wood table, sipping mulled wine that someone had provided. Val inhaled the various scents in the room—cinnamon perfume, minty gum, a Cuban cigar—all mixed with the musky dampness of the walls.

"Everything's clear?" Nora asked.

"Yes," he replied.

She nodded, straightening her elegant shoulders. Peering across the room, she considered the members as they chatted. Perhaps she followed the buzz of conversation. Her intense, chocolate eyes—almost black except for blends of smoky topaz—seemed to assess more than the average person's. Gray at the scalp and graded to black at the ends, her hair gave her a striking appearance.

Bending over the massive oak table, she unrolled the runner stamped with their secret logo, the symbol of an eight-point compass rose shot through with an arrow from south to north. A handful of ravens flew above the west side. She stepped back, then clasped her hands in front of herself.

Nora had been the head of the Council for hundreds of years. Although it wasn't exactly a democracy, the Council ruled by vote. Nora simply had the final say. Luckily, she listened to her advisors.

The Council was the ultimate judicial system in Terror, which took care of the paranormal community. It dealt with matters far beyond those plaguing the normal human world. Issues such as animal instincts, curses, bloodlust, possession, hauntings, and the like were governed by the Paranormal Council, an appointed secret association consisting of a representative from each of the seven major supernatural groups residing in Terror —shifters, vampires, witches, fae, angels, reapers, and ghosts—and a human.

Everyone in Terror knew there was a ruling Council— they just didn't know who was in it. To Nora's right, there was Diego Cruz, a wolf shifter who had come to town from Cuba decades ago. He owned a motorcycle and auto repair shop. The ladies seemed to adore him even though he appeared quite rough around the edges. Next to him was Annabelle Thomas, a faerie princess. She tugged her wavy, blond hair to one side, draping it over her shoulder. Annabelle owned the local bookstore, Fire and Fancy Books. Then there was Nathaniel Newburg, a vampire and bounty hunter. Across the table sat the unearthly contingency: Omar Gamal, the reaper; Sissy LaFleur, an angel with wings the color of champagne; and Simon Jefferies, a ghost who resided in Birkenshire Hall. At the far end, leaning back in his chair as if any one of these supernatural beings wasn't capable of snuffing out his life, sat the council's human representative, Justin Smith.

Val stood off to the side.

Deciding it was time to begin, Nora magically lifted her gavel into the air and slammed it against the table. The group fell silent. The soft clicking sounds of a mouse scuttling along the corners of the room and down the hall reverberated off the stone. The clap of the gavel most likely sent the little creature into a tizzy.

"Good evening," Nora said. "Thank you for joining us." Bracing her palms against the table, she leaned forward. Finished with the formality of welcoming the committee, she got straight to business. "Sheriff Solberg has informed me of escalating tension among the veakling vampire community. Would you care to elaborate, Val?"

"Sure," he said. "Ethan Dunlap has dropped in at the jail every other day, pressuring me to release Payton Grey. He has become more insistent regarding members of this committee and questioning why Ethan is not being released. That's the main reason I took extra precautions concerning this meeting. I wouldn't put it past him to be scouting to unearth the committee."

Ethan had become the leader of the veakling vampires. He seemed to be allowing his newfound popularity to go to his head. The thing was that he had the power to rally the troops. Payton Grey had been arrested last May for underground hustling and hoarding of cobine, a substance vampires needed in the way humans need salt. So far, no one except an undercover operative had linked him to the deed.

"It's a shame it's taken us so long to deal with Payton," Nora commented.

It wasn't an apology for the committee being hung up, but he hadn't expected one. "Given the escalating pressure, a decision to try him or let him go is imperative."

She nodded. "I understand."

"Has anything changed?" Omar spoke up. "Did we receive more evidence that incriminates Payton? If we take another vote, will the outcome be different?" He looked around at the other members.

No one said a word.

Val sighed. "What I've given you so far stands. Payton didn't sell the cobine to anyone in person. Every avenue we've checked leads to a dead end. The only thing we have is the tip someone gave Connor Langley." The stalemate was damned frustrating.

"And the fact the cobine supply has been sporadic," Nathaniel added. "I believe the vampire population is growing more hostile because of the chemical imbalance."

"Which means?" Nora asked.

Nathaniel shrugged. "Riots. Feeding frenzies. More unrest. Who knows? We need Payton to put an end to his control on the cobine market. However he's managing to do it."

Val was aware every supernatural species adapted in some way to live among the population of Terror. It could be a precarious balance for some—such as the vampires and werewolves. Having a supplement such as cobine, manufactured blood, or a donor blood supply could make an otherwise intolerable situation tolerable. "I'm staying on top of this. But unless someone rolls over on him, I doubt we'll get confirmation," Val said.

"Then either find that 'someone' or we need to set him free," Annabelle said.

"Okay," Nathaniel said. "Allow me to speak to Connor one more time. Val, perhaps you can meet the vampire czar along with me. There is something more here. I feel it."

"Many do. That's the reason he's still locked up," Annabelle chimed in.

It was both the curse and the saving grace of being supernatural. Many creatures had a sixth sense when it came to anticipating feelings and outcomes. He didn't possess the gift to the same degree as some others, but he understood it.

Omar and Sissy were the two "not guilty" votes. The reaper and the angel usually saw cases in black or white. For once, though, they mutually agreed Payton Grey should be set free. In such cases, however, a unanimous vote was required since the accused was either banished to an alternate universe or set free.

Nora crossed her arms, her fingers dancing along her tan sleeve. An art deco, diamond-shaped ring glowed on her finger. Small sparks of energy shot from its thumbnail-sized black opal, which was surrounded by diamonds and set in platinum. Val wondered if it were in tune with her emotions because she was clearly aggravated with this dilemma.

"We will give you three more weeks to come up with evidence against Payton, Val, or we let him go," Nora said. "Is everyone in agreement?" She paused, waiting for an objection, but none came. Each member nodded. "So be it."

After asking if there was any other business, she adjourned the meeting with another clap of the gavel.

The members left a couple at a time over several minutes so as not to draw attention on the streets. As always, Val was the last to leave. Keeping a sharp eye out for anything abnormal, he changed into his dragon form and took flight above the city. From there, he could see Diego Cruz duck into his shop. His residence was on the second floor. Other members would be impossible to find because they could trace or vanish to travel across space.

Carrying two baskets filled with flowers and produce from her garden, Twyla McGuire entered Beauty & Beast, her parents' restaurant. Her mother was the beauty and her dad…the beast.

"The only sure things are death and taxes," Ben Gifford said to the man sitting across the table from him. Ben removed his glasses, rubbed each lens on his shirt, and put them back on.

"Not true." Twyla winked as she paused at the end of the table, exchanging a vase of yesterday's sunflowers for new ones. Ben owned a hardware store on the corner of Nevermore Lane and Tenth Street, and he was great about ordering the supplies she needed. Even so, it was midmorning, and she was running later than usual, bringing in the fresh product her parents had ordered.

"Taxes are the only sure thing," she corrected.

Ben grinned. "Is that so?"

"Yep. Just take a stroll in the cemetery come Saturday night. You'll find plenty of undead."

Ben leaned back in the booth. "Don't go all creepy on me, Twyla. It's too early for that." The man across from him snorted before laughing outright.

She chuckled as she moved to the next table, saying over her shoulder, "If you don't like weird stuff, you shouldn't be living in this town, Ben."

"Don't you know that's the attraction? Just anticipating what you may run into, I mean. I suppose it's like that Halloween Horror Night gig they do in Florida. Going there is on my bucket list."

"Good luck." She waved before continuing to the next table.

But she knew that was precisely what drew humans to Terror. The alluring anticipation of encountering a creature from a horror movie and living to tell about it. But the truth was few people who visited Terror remembered their encounters. That was the way the town liked it. The rare humans who weren't susceptible to the memory wash upon leaving the town whispered their intriguing stories. Some humans like Ben even made Terror their home. Although she couldn't imagine why. Terror was perfect for paranormals. Cloaked in secrecy, the town was their sanctuary as long as they lived within its rules. But for humans, Terror often turned into *Close Encounters of the Weird Kind*. She guessed some people got off on that kind of risk. Granted, people enjoyed tempting fate by visiting the town—and hopefully leaving in one piece—and even though it was a lot of shadows and mirrors, there was a real element of danger within the city. It all depended on how well each creature managed to stay in control.

After changing out the flowers on the tables, Twyla headed to the back room. She set the baskets on the side table near the food-prep area. Cook stood in the doorway of a walk-in freezer.

"Nora," Twyla called. Her mother was a calm witch with a significant presence who preferred to be called by her name. Twyla could feel the moment she entered the room. "Oh. There you are."

"Hello, darling," Nora said.

"Here are the veggies I told you about." She strolled over, then gave her mom a quick hug. "I'm not staying. I need to get some root plants in the ground today while the moon is right."

"Okay. Thanks for bringing these by."

Twyla was closer to her mother than her three siblings. Maybe because she strove to please. Solis, the eldest, was extremely independent. Luna, her middle sister, was overly friendly with everyone, yet she butted heads with Nora. But it was her younger brother, Reagan, the only boy, who was baby of the bunch and could do no wrong.

Twyla valued her mother's wisdom. She enjoyed listening and learning, and she wasn't as quick to judge as Solis or as moody as Luna.

Despite their differences, though, she was close to her siblings.

Outside at the curb, she hopped into her red, decked-out UTV—Utility Terrain Vehicle—a Kawasaki Mule with oversized all-terrain tires and a rack on the back that made it easy to haul her plants and gardening supplies around. Several local residents used UTVs or ATVs to get around, especially when the weather was good.

On her way home, she drove two streets over and stopped by Reagan's business, Sacred Skull Drugs. It was one of those quaint, old-fashioned establishments. Luna operated a soda fountain inside. On Tuesdays, her sister made her famous banana dream pie with a peanut-butter and graham-cracker crust. Her mouth watering in anticipation, she decided she'd get a piece to go. Smiling, she wondered if anywhere else in the country still had such a drugstore/soda fountain combination or if anyone under the age of forty would recognize it. This late in the afternoon, she had missed the lunch rush. Luna only served breakfast and lunch, closing the counter at three-thirty.

"Tell me you still have pie," Twyla said as she approached the counter.

Luna neatly folded a towel, then hung it over the oven handle. She made a face, her silver hair falling over one eye. "You're in luck. I made extra today."

"Hot damn." Twyla rubbed her hands together. "I'll be right back. I'm just dropping this with Reagan." She lifted the paper bag she carried. Reagan had asked her to drop off more arrowroot. She found him in his workroom surrounded by beakers and bottles. As a compound pharmacist, he mixed most of his tinctures and medicines by hand.

Twyla rapped on the door, then cracked it open. "Busy?" she asked.

"I have my hands full at the moment," Reagan said. "Just leave it on the table, 'kay?"

"No problem." Twyla dropped the bag on the table. Reagan began pouring a blue liquid into another container of green fluid.

"Thanks."

"You're welcome. Mom said to invite you to dinner on Sunday. So consider yourself invited."

"Gotcha." Reagan squinted, seeming in deep concentration.

Twyla waited until he finished. Once he stepped back from the table, she said, "Reagan, please come this time. It's not the same without you. Who else can make me laugh?"

His mouth lifted in a half-smile. "I don't know. I'm still mad at mom. The matchmaking has gotta stop."

"It's a rite of passage, bro. She'll give up eventually."

Reagan glanced heavenward. "Eventually." He paused, seeming to decide. "Okay. Let Nora know I'll be there."

"Will do." Twyla quietly closed the door. She shoved her hands into her back pockets as she traipsed to the snack counter. When she got there, her sister had a big slice of pie wrapped and waiting for her.

Twyla smiled broadly. "Mmm. You're the best." She lifted the plate, balancing it carefully on her palm. "Nora invited us to dinner Sunday."

"You let Reagan know?"

"Of course. He said he'll come. But that doesn't mean he'll show. You know how he is," she said, rolling her eyes. She knew it depended on her brother's mood at the moment.

Luna shrugged, then said thoughtfully, "Mom and Reagan are getting along better. He might."

"Hmph."

Twyla moved to the doorway to leave as customers entered. She waved as wolf shifters Diego Cruz and Christian Rosewood strolled past. Christian paused. "Hi, Twyla, he said. "I haven't seen you in a while."

"I know. I've been so busy planting and keeping up the garden now the weather is finally warmer."

"We're going to the Freaky Rabbit on Wednesday night for karaoke. You should join us. Like old times." He raised an eyebrow, lifting his chin with a hopeful smile that reminded her of when they'd dated years ago.

"Sounds fun. I might just do that." Her gaze shifted to the side, and she watched Diego travel directly to Luna's counter. He was dressed in his usual black T-shirt, black jeans, and a black leather jacket. His dark, shortly cropped hair and his neatly trimmed beard created a sexy bad-boy look. If she gazed deeply into his coffee eyes, she could see hints of the wolf shifter in him. It probably was no accident Luna was getting off work. They had an on-again-off-again relationship. Evidently, at the moment, they were on. "Maybe I'll drag Luna with me."

"That would be great. We can make it a foursome." He smiled the winsome smile she'd known since they were in fifth grade.

She nodded, then pushed through the doorway.

Outside, Diego's and Christian's bikes were parked next to her "mule." She grinned. One of these days, she may have to get a motorcycle, too. She slid into the mule, then drove home.

Twyla tugged her waist-length hair to one side, then braided the strands down to the ends where she tied it off with a rubber band. Allowing her tresses to tangle all over the place while she tended to her herbs and plants was not something she wanted to deal with, so she always got her hair out of the way first.

She breathed in the aromas of the fragrant flowers and greenery, slipping on leather gloves and lifting the spade. The sun hung low in the west. Clouds were moving in, so the daylight faded quickly. Now that the weather had warmed, she needed to transplant the root plants—turmeric and ginger—from the greenhouse to the raised outside beds.

Opening the arched, wooden greenhouse door, she stepped inside to fetch the wheelbarrow she'd filled with plants earlier that morning. Twyla set her spade inside, then carefully backed the wheelbarrow out the door. She navigated between the rows of raised beds until she arrived at the spot she'd chosen. Kneeling, she went to work preparing the fertile organic soil, breaking apart the rhizomes, and setting them in the ground. When winter returned, she'd repeat the process, housing the plants in the greenhouse during the snowy season.

As she finished and rested on her heels, the sun sank behind a thick row of clouds on the horizon. A rush of cool air washed over her. The hairs on her arms rose, and she had the urge to brush off her skin as if she'd been sprinkled with a light dusting of sand. She stretched to her full height, then turned around.

When she spotted the two vampires who stood within reach, she inhaled sharply. She recognized the closest one. "Ethan, you frightened me. I didn't hear you."

"That was the point."

She cocked her head, her brow furrowing.

Without warning, he tossed a black strap over her and secured it around her waist, latching another tie around her hands, binding them in front of her, then attaching it to the first. She struggled to touch the ruby-red pendant around her neck, which gave her the ability to bend and charm someone to her will, but she couldn't reach it. *Darn it.* Panic gripped her chest.

"What are you doing? Why…"

When he tugged on the lead, she stumbled forward.

"I require your services, my dear," Ethan said. "Do as we ask, and you will be set free in no time."

"Your idea of 'no time' and mine are *not* the same." She heard the hurt and bitterness in her voice and swallowed. He was a neighbor. How could he do this to her? He led her across the yard like a cow. She scuffed her feet, digging her heels in as she went. Twyla thought of the cell phone in her pocket, wondering if there were a way to get in touch with Nora or Luna. Judging from the descending darkness, Reagan had probably already closed the drugstore.

But she didn't have a chance to grab her phone. The rope kept her hands outstretched in front of her, and she winced as it bit into her wrists.

"Son of a bitch." Val Solberg let the blind slat fall back into place before turning toward his office desk. The rumble of the mob's angry voices traveled on the wind.

"What's the matter?" Deputy Trevor, who was also his cousin, asked. With his interest piqued, he let the legs of the chair he'd been teetering on fall to the floor.

"Payton Grey's fan club will be here any second." Val strolled to his desk, then removed a silver stun gun from the bottom drawer.

"Again?"

"Damn. I'll be glad when his trial is over, and we're rid of him."

"Aw, boss, what will we do for entertainment?" Trevor smirked mischievously.

He aimed a piercing glare at his deputy. They had been holding Payton Grey in a cell since last March while the evidence against him was being compiled. A year was a long time to keep anyone contained. But for a vampire, it would be even worse given his magical abilities were curbed, too.

Val's dragon grew restless with the impending confrontation. At times, it was difficult to control his instincts—dragons were born to protect his charges at all costs. As the head of law enforcement in Terror, that instinct was sometimes a double-edged sword. He needed to safeguard the people of the town, but he was also bound to protect the individuals imprisoned in his jail.

He opened the door to the sheriff's office, not bothering to stop it from slamming against the wall of the building. The leader of the vampire group, Ethan Dunlap, stepped onto the walk outside in the snow-dotted yard. There were over twice as many vampires as there had been two weeks ago when they'd last protested. Dunlap brandished his walking cane, its skull-and-snake hilt winking in the streetlights. What weapon was concealed within the cane? A sword or perhaps a poisoned dart? Vampires were cunning and known to hide such weapons.

A roll of smoke wafted from Val's shoulders, similar to the way humans sweated. The scent fortifying him, he took a deep breath and scanned the different breeds of vampires filling the yard. Three designations lived in Terror: old world, turned, and the ones from the planet Cest. Ethan and his coven were veaklings, a young cluster of turned vampires who usually attained blood groupies as donors in exchange for financial and living support—a place to stay or food. Half-a-dozen vamps, give or take, in the community were phlebotomists. All breeds used them at one time or another.

Val snorted. As long as no one showed up dead, they were good.

Crossing his arms, he stood firm. "We've been through this, Ethan. You and your…group can head back the way you came. Grey will remain in custody until he's convicted or cleared."

Ethan kept moving toward Val. "You need to reveal the Council members. We have the right to speak to them."

"No. You don't," Val said, tone flat. Ethan's sense of entitlement was getting old.

"Payton's case has gone on for far too long. There are extenuating circumstances, and his family needs him home," Ethan shouted.

The main problem Val could distinguish was a sense of desperation among the group. If he had to guess, he'd say these vamps were desperate to get their hands on the cobine Payton Grey had been accused of black-marketing. Val didn't think their concern was for Grey, but themselves.

Perhaps Ethan was feeling pressure due to Connor Langley's presence in town. The vampire czar had arrived the night before.

The mass of thirty or so vampires closed ranks, then an aisle parted the center. Two males escorted a female to the front. As they neared, Val sucked in a breath. Two men led Twyla McGuire toward him, her hands tied in front of her and a length of leather strapped around her waist.

Anger surged through Val, flaming hot. He hadn't been able to meet her expectations years ago when they'd been together, but that didn't mean he hadn't loved her. They'd simply had different life goals and responsibilities back then. The sight of her at the mercy of Ethan and his vamp gang nearly undid him.

"Let her go," Val ordered.

"All in due time. If she cooperates." Ethan lifted his chin with a snarl. "My sources say her mother is the one who placed the collar around Payton's neck—the one with a Capture Stone that keeps him captive and unable to trace. If that's true, then I'm counting on dear Mom to trade Payton's freedom for her daughter's."

Tossing her head back, Twyla laughed throatily. "Well, you've been misinformed, Ethan. It's not a Capture Stone. It's a Ruin Coin."

"Twyla." The muscles along Val's back tightened. He shook his head slightly, willing her to keep her mouth shut. At the same time, he knew she wouldn't. Holding back wasn't Twyla's style, not when she was angered. And when she was…whoever was on the receiving end better look out.

"My mother isn't the one who cast a spell on the Ruin Coin. I am."

Ethan scowled. "Then you can undo it."

"Hardly."

Clenching and unclenching his fist, Ethan marched over to Twyla. Placing his fingers at her throat, he applied downward pressure, forcing her to kneel. Over his shoulder, he ordered his followers, "Bring me, Nora, now. The art of *persuasion* works both ways."

"*Stop,*" Val bellowed when several vampires started to follow their master's command. The coil of smoke coming off Val increased. "This is *not* how we address issues in Terror. Go home. I've personally spoken with the committee. They are aware of the length of time Payton has been held, and their final decision will be handed down soon."

Gripping her tightly by the arm, Ethan dragged Twyla up from where she knelt.

"Now release her," Val bit out. He had reached his breaking point. Trying to control the shift, he took a deep breath as he changed into his dragon form. Scales rippled along his back, chest, and arms. His legs and body grew exponentially, claiming the entirety of the space between the walkway and the jail, the triangular tip of his tail just touching the porch. When he expelled a roar, fire surged out of his mighty jaws.

Val charged forward.

Ethan swung his cane at Twyla, clipping her head just above her ear. She crumpled to the ground, unconscious. A millisecond later, Val's massive dragon form knelt at her side. Using his claws, he quickly but delicately undid the loops around her wrists. When the leather binding dropped away, he scooped her up, settling her into the crook of his scaly arm. Loosing yet another fiery roar, he flew into the air.

From the ground, Ethan's furious shout of, "*No*," reverberated through the crowd. *The insane vampire must not realize how fortunate he is,* Val thought darkly. If Twyla hadn't been in the middle of the mob, he would have scorched the entire lot. He couldn't believe they'd dared to use her as a pawn. Fury burning so bright hot in his chest, he took another pass at the vampires, releasing a fiery blaze with a snarled exhale. Luckily for the veaklings, they could move at lightning-fast speeds. The traitors were able to dodge the flames, pushing their ranks back.

Ethan followed his colleagues, tracing a safe distance from Val's dragon form.

Leave now and don't ever return, Val growled, throwing his thoughts at the group.

He didn't wait to see if they complied. If they dared to defy him, it would start a war between other supernaturals and their kind. Surely vampire veaklings weren't that foolish. Still, he made another pass above the group, soaring above them as they traced out of sight. When the roadway cleared, he flew to his home, Thurston Mansion, on the northern edge of town. He occupied the east wing while Trevor lived in the west with some friends. The Angel Alliance, the original residents of Terror, had the main section of Thurston Manor.

Landing in the mammoth entrance of the courtyard, Val gently lay Twyla down before shifting into his human form. Taking the time to calm his breathing, he knelt, lifted Twyla, and held her unconscious form across his thighs. Her breathing was shallow, her eyes closed, and her head lolled limply.

Apprehension stabbed his gut. "Twyla, are you okay?" he asked.

She moaned slightly, but she didn't wake. His worry growing, he used gentle fingers to examine the wound above her ear. Blood oozed from two pinhole marks, which rose from a purplish, swollen knot almost hidden by her hair. The mark resembled a snake bite. Had the hilt of Ethan's cane contained poison? He took a deep breath. Twyla was a witch, but snake venom would kill her just as it would a human.

When her breath stuttered, his stomach dropped. He needed to take her to David Snyder, the principal angel at the Alliance. Val suspected the angel had abilities beyond what could even be imagined. Given they were in the angel compound, it was also Twyla's best chance.

Rising with her in his arms, Val hurried toward the entrance. The double doors opened before he could ring the bell, which wasn't a surprise because the staff would be monitoring the security cameras from inside.

"What happened?" the butler, Grady, asked as he stepped back to let Val enter, then rushed to close it behind him.

"There was a veakling uprising, and Twyla got caught in the middle of it," Val said. "I need David."

Grady nodded, although his mouth tugged to one side in what could have been displeasure or even indecision. "Take her into the salon."

The sound of the butler's footsteps on the marble floor as he exited mingled with Val's own as he entered a large room down the hall and to the right of the main entrance. He gently placed Twyla on the sofa, then perched beside her on the edge of the seat. This time, she didn't make a sound or stir at all.

He lifted her hand, then ran his thumb over her delicate blue veins. Her skin felt icy, and he needed to get her warm. Rising, he made his way over to the fireplace. Calling on his dragon, he blew flames over the logs, igniting them into a roaring fire.

That might help.

He paced the room, glancing at Twyla on every other pass.

Soon after, the butler entered with David on his heels. A few seconds later, Seth, an archangel from outside of Terror, stepped into view and leaned against the doorjamb, folding his arms.

Great, David has company.

Whenever Seth visited Terror, which was around a dozen times a year, he stayed in the mansion. It was where all the angels assembled—an angel compound of sorts. The colossal mansion could hold many visitors, so guests weren't a problem. Heck, technically, Val was a guest. Angels and dragons had an interlinked relationship of shared wisdom and protection. Where one was found, the other was often as well.

"What have we here?" David asked.

Val marched over, then dropped to one knee beside Twyla. He smoothed her hair. "Ethan struck her in the head with his walking stick. I fear it somehow delivered a dose of snake poison."

David came closer, bending to examine the wound.

"Good catch, my man. I believe you're right."

Seth joined them, waiting for David to move so he could see.

"Yes. Those twin fang punctures do resemble a snake's."

"Will you draw it out of her?" Val asked.

David gave a curt nod. Placing his forefingers over the oozing pinholes above Twyla's ear, he slowly moved his hand back, coaxing two greenish-yellow threads of liquid out. When the threads reached about four inches in length, he jerked his hand backward, tugging and separating the streams from her scalp and catching the poison in his hand.

"Excellent job," Seth said, then smiled knowingly. "I guess you've done that before."

A low rumble escaped David's throat. "A time or two." The threads in his hand glowed and vaporized.

"Will she be okay?" Val asked, unable to control the worry swirling inside him.

"Time will tell," David replied with unnerving calm. "We'll know more tomorrow. Let her rest in the purple room by your quarters. That way, so you can periodically check in on her."

Val nodded, then stood. "I hope she recovers."

"Yeah. I'd hate to be the one to inform Nora something happened to her daughter," David said.

Val's heart ached at the thought of Twyla dying. He couldn't imagine living his life knowing she wouldn't be there when he was ready to commit. He'd always felt like they'd try again someday—when their lives were more in sync. He swallowed hard. What if he'd thrown away the few years they could have had? And for what... stubbornness?

"Val." Seth's voice penetrated Val's thoughts. He glanced up at the archangel, whose veil of black dreads hid his eyes. "David asked what happened."

"Sorry. I got lost in thought," Val said. "These veakling altercations have gotten out of hand. Ethan took Twyla hostage to persuade me, and her mother, to release Payton Grey."

Sissy LaFleur strolled by the salon, hesitated, then came inside. "I heard you mention Payton Grey. We just discussed him at the Council meeting. Anything new?"

"Yes. No. Ethan and his veakling gang are still at odds with the Council," Val replied.

"Well, we can put him in jail, too," Sissy snapped.

David, always the diplomat, held up his hand. "Wait. Surely, they realize they're breaking the law, right? We'll wait to see how Twyla's recovery goes, then deal with them accordingly. If she dies…."

Val glared, unwilling to consider the possibility she

wouldn't pull through. He thought to argue, his desire for justice bubbling at the surface, but he needed to take Twyla to her room. "A decision can be made tomorrow." He bent, lifting Twyla into his arms, then straightened. "If you'll excuse me, I'll see that she gets her rest."

The three angels watched him until he reached the door. Once he was outside, he heard them break into an escalating argument. *Whatever.* Caring for Twyla was more important.

The purple room was located down another short hallway off to the left, in the opposite direction of his quarters. Once he entered the room, he tugged down the comforter before laying her on the four-poster bed. She didn't stir. A thrum of worry vibrated through him. He'd seen David extract the poison with his own eyes, but that alone wouldn't make her magically better. A lot depended on her ability to fight whatever poison had worked its way into her system. He tried to calm his racing thoughts. *She'll wake up,* he reassured himself, desperately clinging to that bit of hope.

After pulling off her shoes to make her as comfortable as he could, he tucked the covers around her and kissed her forehead. Leaving a dim lamp on, he shut the door behind himself on the way out, wincing at the finality of the *clicking* sound.

*

From out of a deep haze, Twyla felt something brush her face. It was wet...and fuzzy. Her nose tickled, and she scrunched up her face. Then something pawed at her chest.

Yelping, she tried to push up onto her elbows. With heavy lids, she peeked her eyes open as something hairy ran over her legs. Then human footsteps pounded toward her. She rubbed her knuckles across her eyes, then blinked.

David?

She recognized the angel's hickory-brown hair with platinum streaks. Flipping his hair back, he revealed the scar that slashed across his beautiful face and came to an abrupt halt. "Prissy, come here," he rasped at his pup, obviously trying to whisper so as not to disturb her.

Too late. Prissy had already accomplished that.

Twyla struggled to sit up. Her head throbbed. Actually, every part of her ached, especially her neck and shoulders.

David made kissy sounds at the dog. "Prissy, come here." Then, to Twyla, he said, "I'm sorry. I think she heard you moan."

"I don't moan," Twyla said.

"I beg to differ."

She waved a hand. "It doesn't matter." She'd seen David around town with his dogs a few times, although he seemed different at the moment…less guarded.

He tromped farther into the room. "Prissy, let's go." He went to pick up the pup, but she dodged to the side, obviously making a game out of catching her.

Twyla glanced around, suddenly realizing she was in a strange bed in an unfamiliar room. "Where am I…and, what am I doing here?"

"You had an altercation with a vampire. He struck you with his poison-laced walking cane. Val brought you to the compound."

Surprised, she furrowed her brow as she fought to remember. "How long…?"

"You've been here for two days. Val has been quite worried."

Twyla sat on the edge of the bed. She fought the wooziness that crashed over her, leaning to one side, then tightening the muscles along the spine for control. "What about my mother?"

"Val contacted her, and she came to check on you once."

She didn't recall Nora among the few glimmers of hazy memories.

Finally, David caught Prissy. The pup waved its front paws up and down, begging for something, perhaps to be petted, as he nestled her in the crook of his arm. "We'll find you a treat," he murmured, then moved toward the door, saying over his shoulder, "I'll let Val know you're awake."

A fresh set of clothes were folded neatly on the massive bathroom counter, a stretch of marble from one wall to the other with two sinks. Her mother must have brought them when she stopped by.

It was Thursday, Twyla thought fuzzily. She'd lost two days. Darn Ethan Dunlap and his vampires.

She cleaned up, using the rosemary-and-mint soap in the shower. It wasn't the best shower she'd ever had, but it was close to it. Drying with an oversized white towel, she rubbed feeling back into her body. Did angels do everything on such a large scale? She squinted at her reflection in the gold-framed mirror. The curve above her ear was a purplish bruise. Wincing, she smoothed her hair over her ears with her fingers, leaving it in a damp tangle down her back.

She dressed in her own clothes, but, oddly, she still felt like someone else. Her rubber gardening boots with the floral design were by the door. They didn't go with her black-and-white pinstriped pants. With a sigh, she stepped into a hall and made her way into the foyer, looking for someone who could take her home.

Val entered the foyer, watching Twyla pause to examine a painting of a boy on a boat. She had a curiosity about her that he had always liked. "There's a lot of nice artwork in this place," she commented.

"The angels are well-traveled patrons of the arts," he said.

"That's obvious." She glanced over her shoulder, her face brightening.

"You like paintings," Val said.

She laughed, seeming shocked he remembered. "Yes. I'm not a very good judge of what's good or not. I'm particularly fond of oils, though. They seem to have an earthiness about them."

"I know what you mean," he said. He liked the dense texture of oils. "I hadn't given much thought to who had placed the Ruin Coin on Payton. I was in St. Paul when that happened. I guess Trevor and Nate were in the office then."

Apparently, Val had caught her off guard. She whipped around, settling her gaze on him. "Yes, I put it on, Payton. And you're right. You weren't here. Nora and I take turns doing those mundane tasks, and it was my turn."

Val nodded. A Ruin Coin was a standard police procedure when a supernatural was arrested. It was a means to nullify magical powers temporarily. "In that case, it might be better if you hung out here for a while. Either that or I can keep tabs on your place. I don't think Ethan will give up easily."

She crossed her arms. "I can take care of myself."

"Like you did when he captured you?" Val asked with a raised brow.

"I wasn't prepared then. Now I will be."

She had a stubborn streak the size of the Mississippi River. "You will most likely be outnumbered. That's how the veaklings operate."

"I can put a protection spell on my house."

"And if you're at the drugstore, the bank, or at Caffeinated Corpse's Cappuccino?" He inhaled, intending to say more, but his thoughts were captured in her sweet scent. It was the smell of the soap the angels used in the mansion altered by her fragrance. Val gave himself a mental shake. He had never truly gotten over her.

"I'll deal with it," she ground out.

That wasn't good enough for him. For heaven's sake, only two days had passed since she'd been tied up, struck down, and poisoned. Did she have a death wish?

Grudgingly, he said, "Whatever."

She let her hands fall, her shoulders relaxing. "Thanks."

"I'll drive you home."

"I'd appreciate that."

Prissy came darting through the foyer, chasing her sister, Ruby, and scampered right between Val and Twyla. Tank, a big sweetheart of a Rottweiler halted dutifully at the doorway, looking in. Hastily, she jerked back to avoid the dogs. Her booted foot gripped the floor tile, holding her in place while the rest of her body tipped. He slid his hand around her waist to steady her, and her softness nudged his memory. The next thing he knew, he turned and captured her mouth with his.

He kissed her, hard at first, a build-up of all the times he'd thought about kissing her over the years but hadn't. Then he circled his arms around her and pulled her against him, gentling the pressure of his lips, paying attention to her response. She threaded her hands into his hair, holding him close until he broke the kiss. They stood there for a long moment, his forehead pressed to hers, their breath mingling as he felt her rapid pulse slow.

"Let me watch over you?" he asked—almost begged— his voice a murmur.

"I'm thinking of a guardian with benefits," she said, twisting slightly as she smiled against his cheek.

"I like benefits. But that may land us in a world of hurt again." He wasn't prepared to get his heart entangled a second time. And he knew what would happen if he gave it a chance.

With a peal of yippy barking, the dogs shot a path out of the bedroom, joined by the clack of Tank's heavier plodding footsteps as they headed for the kitchen. David was probably fixing lunch for his guest. Seth loved food. If he weren't an angel, he'd no doubt weigh four hundred pounds, judging by his dining habits alone.

He steered Twyla toward the double doors. They exited the mansion with his arm still around her.

"I should say goodbye and offer my thanks," she said, pausing at his Jeep.

"I'll relay your message. David is probably tied up with Seth, anyway." He scowled at his choice of words. "You know how guests are."

He opened the door for her, and she climbed in. "Yeah. I suppose." She glanced back at the mansion, uncertainty on her face.

Was she having second thoughts about leaving? He shut the door, and she clicked her seat belt.

He took the same route into town as always, but it felt like a different journey today. For one thing, his renewed desire for Twyla had been unexpected. For another, he wasn't kidding that he was concerned for her safety. Something was in the air. Perhaps even more than a veakling uprising. He just couldn't put his finger on it. Dragons were loyal, solid, tunnel-vision types. Perhaps he should seek out a seer for some advice.

Twyla's place was on the other side of town from his. He glanced at the sun, which was high in the sky. "Do you want to stop for lunch before I take you home?"

"Sure. I'm starved."

*

Twyla chose Fire & Fuel Eatery for lunch, which was known for its spicy food and casual outdoor patio. Her lovely garden boots weren't what she'd normally wear around town, but hunger trumped fashion.

Besides, everyone in town knew she was spontaneous, sassy, straight-forward, and a risk-taker. And that she and Val had a relationship a few years ago. Not that she cared what people thought. She glanced at him, already soothed by his baritone voice and commanding presence and the concern she found in his eyes.

She and Val grabbed a wooden picnic table near the edge of the patio. She could see over the black wrought iron fence and hedge as people strolled by. The foot traffic had picked up now that summer had arrived. Terror didn't solicit and encourage visitors, though. It was a close-knit, private town that appreciated its neighbors, but outsiders weren't all that welcome.

They came here, anyway—people searching for the thrill of danger. Thank goodness the glamour placed on the town kept the true nature of Terror hidden from human eyes. Very few saw the real Terror.

She picked up the menu tucked in by the condiments and napkins. One side listed the human entrees. She flipped it over to the paranormal side, which was written in the same magical ink that was used throughout town. They offered something for just about everyone, from vamp beverages made with dried blood powder to raw fish catering to kelpies to sausage on a hoagie roll for the average Joe.

The waitress came over sporting a Fire & Fuel T-shirt, her fairy wings protruding from slits in the fabric. "Hey, there. What can I get you?" She flashed a smile, shifting from side to side as if she had excess fairy energy.

Val ordered a beer, and she asked for a glass of water with lime.

"And for lunch?" the waitress asked.

"Go ahead," Val said to Twyla.

She looked up from her menu. "I'll have the blue-cheese-and-bacon-stuffed-dates and Lacinato kale."

"Okay. And for you, Val?" the waitress asked. "Your usual?"

"Yes. Bratwurst and potatoes, thanks. No bread, no greens, and none of that fancy stuff."

She smiled. "All righty. Be back in a flash."

"You know," he started.

Twyla rolled her eyes. He was going into lecture mode.

"Wait, listen," he said. "If you're going to go out, this is the time of day to do it. High noon. A vamp would need a strong reason to be running around in full daylight."

He was right. But she already knew that. They probably wouldn't bother her when the sun was at its zenith. It all depended on the vampire's ancestral makeup. All were sensitive to sunlight to some degree, but it wasn't merely the daylight itself that kept them from day-walking. Depending on their lineage, some vamps came and went during the early morning and late-afternoon hours, avoiding direct overhead sunlight; other vamps were too light-sensitive to risk going out at all. She'd heard of vampires purchasing charms and spells to make day-walking safer, but neither she nor Nora offered that service. It was very risky. If something went wrong, it could kill someone.

"Yes. I know," she said.

Their waitress delivered their drinks, and the meal came a few minutes later. That was the cool thing about lunch—they were fast. She unrolled her setting, set the silverware aside, and arranged the napkin on her lap.

When she glanced back up, two figures stood beside their table—Christian and Diego.

"Hey," Christian said. "Wow, imagine running into each other two times in one week. The universe is trying to tell us something." Nervously, he peered between Val and Twyla. "I…we…missed you last night at the Freaky Rabbit. Change your mind?"

"Not exactly." She laughed. "I got tied up, and I couldn't get away." She exchanged a glimpse with Val at the truth behind her explanation.

Christian nodded. "Those brats look good. I may get that."

Diego nudged Christian from behind. "Not if we don't grab a table." As they moved on, he said over his shoulder to Twyla, "Say hi to Luna for me." Then he pointed at a table in the back. "How about over there?"

Twyla's gaze met Val's glare. "I'm sorry your plans got squashed," he quietly said in a tone that didn't match his eyes. The corner of his mouth curled up in a knowing smirk.

Okay, now she was confused. What was she missing? The only thing she could think about was the kiss they'd shared earlier. It had sparked a renewed fire in her. Had it done the same for him?

They finished their lunch, barely speaking.

He drove her home, then walked her to the door. He'd been foolish by allowing his emotions to get to him. A relationship hadn't worked before, so why should he think it would be any different now?

Reaching the veranda, Twyla sucked air into her lungs. Val followed her gaze to see what had startled her. There was a mark on the door. An *X* with a swish of three slashes through the upper axis—made in blood.

"A death mark," he murmured. He grabbed her arm, drawing her back. "You're not staying here."

"It's nothing," she said. "I was just surprised, that's all. I'm not afraid of some streak on my door."

"Ethan is issuing another warning."

"He's merely trying to scare me."

"I don't want you staying here alone."

She rolled her eyes. "Then stay. It's fine with me if you do."

He had the extra help at the jail arranged already, and they had moved Payton Grey deeper into an underground cell. So he had things covered in that respect, too. No one would be breaking Payton out. Trevor was dedicated and fierce when provoked.

Val's gaze swept the grounds, noting how vulnerable she was. "Anyone could trace in here."

"It's a home, not a compound."

"Let's go to my place," he said.

"I don't think that's necessary." Her mouth quirked upward in resignation, but she turned back to the entrance. "But let me get a few things, and we can go."

Twenty minutes later, he escorted her safely into his living room. She strolled over to the seating arrangement, then she threw herself into his butter-soft leather recliner. "I'd forgotten how much I love this chair."

He wanted to ask, *Just the chair?* Instead, he clamped his lips together. He set her bag down. Remembering his manners, he inquired, "Would you like something to drink?"

Twyla glanced up, her midnight hair spilling over her shoulders. Her long lashes swept down and then up as her dark eyes appealed to him. "Surprise me."

Did she know what she was asking? Or better yet, how his mind and body would interpret the invitation? "You're much too trusting, Twyla."

She closed her eyes with a moan. "Uh-huh."

Shaking his head, he went to the kitchen. He opened the refrigerator, searching for something she'd like. She probably needed rest and energy given she was still recovering from being knocked out for two days. With her health in mind, he grabbed a smoothie full of vitamins, fruits, and vegetables. He hoped it hadn't been in there too long. His housekeeper bought them from time to time, hoping he'd eat better. It hadn't worked so far.

He returned to the living room, holding the beverage out for her. "Your drink."

"You'd make a horrible waiter."

He shot her a mock-hurt expression. "I'm talented at many things."

"Being a servant isn't one of them." She took the drink, twisted the cap off, and took a sip.

"I got you a drink, didn't I?" he countered.

She laughed. "You did."

"There you go."

"Well?" Tilting her head, she stared into his eyes, then blinked. "Oh, I don't know. I lost my train of thought."

He wondered at her distraction, hoping it wasn't a residual effect from her head injury or the poison.

She downed the drink, then seemed to consider. "You're much better with weapons."

"Noted." He sat in a recliner a few feet away. Taking out his cell phone, he sent David and Nate, the Council's vampire rep, text messages telling them what happened and asking if they wanted to stop by his house at midnight to discuss the situation. They agreed.

When he looked up, he noticed Twyla peering at him suspiciously.

"I was updating David," he said.

Her lips tugged to one side. "I guess he'd want to know. I mean, the angels have their fingers on everything that goes on in town."

"Your incident and the mark on your house may influence the Council to act faster."

"Do you think so? I don't mind helping law enforcement by putting a holding spell on someone, but when someone attacks me, that's going too far." She yawned, then tucked her legs underneath herself.

"Why don't you go to bed?" he suggested. "Your body is still recovering."

She twisted her neck. Touching her fingertips to her head, she winced. "You're probably right."

"See, you agreed with me. I knew you weren't your normal self yet."

She smiled. His chest grew heavy, right along with his heartbeat.

"Of course I agree with you. I'm not crazy."

She closed her eyes as she settled deeper into the chair. He longed to scoop her into his lap, stroke the loose strands of hair at her temple.

She jerked, waking. "I think I will go to bed." Standing, she wobbled. "Ooh."

With a few quick steps, he grabbed her by the elbow. It was difficult to resist the urge to draw her into his arms, especially as she leaned on him and placed her cheek against his chest.

"It may take several days for the effect of the poison to be completely gone," he said. "I'll show you to the guest room."

"Okay," she whispered into his shirt. She didn't seem in any hurry to move, shuffling her feet as he guided her around the coffee table and the other side of the seating arrangement. Once the fatigue started to set in, it knocked her for a loop. Good thing he hadn't offered her an alcoholic drink. In he had, she'd probably be down for the count.

The guest rooms, along with his bedroom, were upstairs. He slipped his arm around her as they ascended. It seemed to take great effort for her to climb the steps. Feeling bad for her, he gave in, lifting her into his arms and carrying her the remainder of the distance.

"It's not our honeymoon," she groaned huskily.

"You would know it if it were," he assured her, his voice thickening.

She lifted her head, peering at him from under her eyelids.

When he arrived at her room, he kicked the door open with his foot, then took her directly to the bed and placed her on top of the heavy quilt. He hadn't had the maid change the comforter in the guest rooms to lighter linens as he usually did in the spring—an oversight due to the extra hours he'd been spending at the office.

She rolled away from him, curling up the way she often did. He watched her for a long moment, wondering if something in the smoothie he'd given her could have reacted with any residual poison in her system. Or perhaps she was sensitive to an ingredient. Or maybe she was just exhausted. But she had fizzled out so quickly that it concerned him.

Since she was dressed, he didn't bother with the covers. He left her to sleep, then went to retrieve her belongings. When he returned, he set the bag on the chair. She hadn't moved an inch.

After tucking her hair behind her ear, he quietly left, then closed the door. He checked his watch. It was only ten-thirty. David and Nate would arrive in an hour and a half—plenty of time for a quick shower to wash away Twyla's scent. He inhaled as he walked down the hall to his room. Her fragrance on his clothes and skin teased him, and it wouldn't let go.

In his bathroom, Val kicked off his shoes next to the double-sink vanity. Reaching in, he turned on the shower as hot as it would go. It couldn't begin to touch his dragon's heat. He stripped, dropped his clothes on the floor, and stepped beneath the forceful spray.

Good. So good.

He tipped his head back. Letting the water run through his hair, he reveled in the soothing warmth of it over his tense shoulders and down his abs. He stood there until the water began to cool, allowing the water to beat against his tired muscles. But it wouldn't drive away his doubts and fears. Finally, he washed, dried, and dressed in fresh clothes.

The master bedroom was downstairs, situated behind the living room and a wall that housed a large fireplace and concealed wall that held firearms. Tiptoeing, he angled his head, listening for any indication Twyla had roused.

Time for a drink.

He was almost to the bar when the doorbell rang. David or Nate must have arrived early. He abruptly changed direction, intending to reach the door before they rang again and woke Twyla.

He yanked the door open, but neither David nor Nate greeted him. Nora stood in the entry, her arms crossed. Twyla's mom looked like a mama bear protecting her cub.

"Twyla is here, right? Is she okay? The last time I saw her, she was unconscious. When I stopped by her house, I saw the marks."

Finally, she stopped fussing, and he could get a word in. "She's fine. She's sleeping in the guest room. Would you like to come in?" he asked, feeling a bit put out she had shown up on his doorstep. It hadn't escaped him that David and Nate would be there any minute. Nora would soon realize he hadn't invited her to the spur-of-the-moment meeting. With Twyla involved, the witch was too close to the situation. Now he'd have little choice but to include her.

"Yes. Thank you." She stepped across the threshold. "May I see her?"

He pursed his lips, then said, "She's sleeping. But if you must, the room is upstairs on the right."

She squinted at him curiously. Maybe it was because he made no move to escort her.

"David and Jake will be here shortly to discuss the latest implication of the mark on her home." There was no sense of hiding it from her. They would be here any minute.

"The three of you are meeting outside of the Paranormal Council?" she asked sharply.

"The sudden turn of events warrants a discussion," he said, his voice terse. "It's for Twyla's safety. I could act alone, but I'm afraid the community may not like my solution." He gave a sarcastic smile.

"You should have called me."

Val shook his head. "You are too close to the situation."

"Snake balls," she snapped. "I'm as impartial as the next person."

He choked out a laugh. "Right. But snakes don't have balls."

"That depends on if the snake is a vampire. In that case, I'll twist them right off." She cupped her hand in the air. As if she were plucking a plum, she wrenched her hand and made a popping sound with her tongue.

He shuddered. Then the doorbell rang a second time, and the clock on the mantle struck midnight.

The evening hadn't gone as planned since leaving the angel's sanctuary, and apprehension whisked through him as he ushered them inside.

As they were heading to the living room to sit when his back was turned, David lifted a brow and angled his head toward Nora, as if wondering why she was there. Val had said it would just be the three of them.

Val ignored him. "Anyone want a drink?" He still hadn't made it to the bar.

"Bourbon," David said.

"Me too," Nate added.

"Same," Nora chimed in. The men glanced at her, seeming surprised by her choice. "I happen to like whiskey," she said defensively, inclining her head and allowing the black tips of her hair to fall back over her shoulders.

Val fixed the drinks, then distributed them. Silence hung in the air as they consumed beverages. But Val didn't sit. Instead, he chose to pace. He went back and forth along the open side of the seating arrangement three times, contemplating where to begin. Pausing, he tipped his glass and took a long swallow, almost finishing his bourbon. "I believe we have an even bigger problem. I don't think the veaklings are working alone. The stain on Twyla's door had three claw marks on it…made by a demon."

Nora sucked in a sharp breath. "I hope you're wrong."

"Consider this…" Val launched into the summary as he knew it. "Payton Grey has been in jail for a year. In the beginning, he was a little-known veakling. He wasn't on our radar at all until Connor Langley asked for our help, then brought Payton to the Council's attention. We've kept him locked up because the evidence has been conflicting. Connor had indicated smuggling and black-marketing the cobine. Whenever we find evidence, someone comes forward to contradict it. The veakling uprising has steadily grown, and now we have this mark… Perhaps they've gotten cocky, and they've revealed the true identity behind our problems. Perhaps the mastermind behind the veaklings is a demon."

The group glanced at one another, each trying to judge what the other thought. Val stood near the mantle, a large flat-screen TV at his back.

"That's a whole new ballgame," David said.

"Why?" Nate finished the last of his drink, then set the tumbler on the end table. "Why would they get involved with vampires?"

"Brindles and broomsticks, the lower demons don't act alone. This could run much deeper than we first imagined." Nora stood and strolled to the stone fireplace, staring at the ashes as if searching for a clue there.

"But Nate is right—we need to find out why they are getting involved in Terror," David said, shaking his head.

"It seems to have something to do with Payton Grey and the fact Twyla confined the vampire's powers, which allows us to keep him in jail," Val added.

"Payton, cobine, a smuggling ring—that's what we're aware of," Nate said.

Nora turned a piercing gaze on them. "And Twyla is tied to him because she helped the law and the Council keep Payton under wraps."

Val pounded his fist into the palm of his other hand. "By dragon's blood, I will not allow a demon to hurt someone I care about." And he cared about Twyla more than he wanted to admit.

David raised a brow.

"I knew you hadn't gotten over her," Nora chortled. "My readings are always unclear regarding my children, but there have been hints about you two."

Val shot her a glare.

"Don't worry. I won't say anything to her," Nora said, a small smile playing on her lips.

"Okay. Let's get back on subject," David advised. "What do you propose we do about the demons? We should inform the rest of the Council, but I suggest we develop a plan before we tell them."

From the direction of the curved staircase came Twyla's raspy voice. "What's this about demons?"

Val pivoted toward her voice. Twyla traveled gracefully down the last few steps, past the glass dining table, and into the living area. She looked beautiful with her black hair flowing over her shoulders and her eyes heavy from sleep. Stopping near him, she took in the group, including her mother.

Nora sighed dramatically. "At least those vampires didn't bite you, dear." To Nate, she added, "No offense."

He shrugged. "None taken."

"I'm sorry we woke you," Val said.

"You didn't. I've had more than enough sleep. And…it was Payton who woke me. He called from his cell. He said something about piranha teeth."

Nora threw her hands in the air. "That's so odd, it's absurd."

A murmured agreement came from the room.

"I do think Payton is the place to start," David said. "See if he'll reveal anything about the demons."

"I was thinking the same thing," Val agreed.

Twyla sidled up beside him, turning her golden eyes on his face. "I'll go with you."

"No. Not until we have a better idea of what is going on."

"I can tell you that. What the demons want, I mean," Nora said. "They're searching for a way to multiply."

"You mean have babies?" Val said, his voice rising with incredulous disbelief.

"That's exactly what I mean. They weren't too happy when I turned them down," Nora added.

6

"Are you claustrophobic?" Val asked.

"No. I don't think so," Twyla answered. But ten minutes later, she discovered she'd been wrong. *So wrong!* She followed Val through one twist after another as they moved along the carved-out rock passageway. Her heartbeat sped up, and her blood pounded in her ears. If she removed her shirt, she'd probably be able to wring out a gallon of sweat. Evidently, she wasn't a fan of narrow, confined spaces. Who knew?

The jail Payton Grey was held in was deeper underground than she'd expected. "You need an elevator down to this place," she said. They had been in the sheriff's office when she'd placed the Ruin Coin on Payton, so she hadn't been privy to his accommodations.

At last, they entered a large hall with a couple of doors. Val unlocked one, then ushered her inside an even bigger vestibule.

Lights automatically came on. "Motion detectors?" she asked.

"Yes." He guided her to another locked door.

"Holey-moley, you take security seriously," she said.

He nodded. "Paranormal creatures aren't like humans. It is my job to protect our citizens as best I can." He placed a finger on a digital print reader, and the mechanism clicked its confirmation of his identity. "Stay here," he said over his shoulder. "Let me check on him first." The door opened soundlessly, and Val stepped inside.

Twyla was right on his heels. If something were going on, she wanted to know what it was.

He sighed. "Do you ever do as you're told?"

She didn't answer. Instead, she shot him a saucy smile.

On the other side of the door, the space opened into a spacious room comprised of a kitchen and living room with a wall-mounted TV at one end. It seemed to have all the comforts of home, which was more than Payton deserved.

Speaking of…

He lounged in a huge, black recliner. "Oh, look, Doris. We have company," he said with mock interest.

Doris, a steel-gray cat, popped her head up from behind a pillow. She arched her back, staring at them with blue-green eyes. Val moved closer. Doris hissed and sputtered, showing her pointy white teeth.

Classical music played in the background, which was an odd contradiction to the disgust on Payton's face. "To what do I owe this pleasure?" he asked.

When he spotted Twyla a step behind Val, Payton's eyes widened. He hurriedly lowered the chair, straightening his spine.

She hadn't seen him since she'd placed the Ruin Coin on him.

"Are you going to remove this hex and free me?" His voice sounded hopeful.

"No," Val bit out. "But perhaps soon…*if* you cooperate."

"And you have to convince me," Twyla said.

Payton sneered. "What is it you want from me?"

"There is someone else behind your cobine dealings. Who is it?" Val moved farther into the room to stand in front of Payton. Twyla followed.

Payton stroked the cat. "Go blow some smoke, dragon. There's no one. And I wasn't running cobine, to begin with."

"No. I think you were hoarding it," Val accused. "Stockpiling it to drive up the price."

Val and Nate had mentioned their theory to the Council, but they hadn't been able to find where he had hidden the cobine. They only knew there was a shortage they couldn't account for. It seemed the deficit had a domino effect, eliciting an aggressive behavior within the vampire community.

They hadn't found any connections to pin on Payton.

Twyla glanced sideways at Val. "Wait, did you see that? He stroked the cat with the first answer, but not the second. Could that be a tell? A subconscious movement."

Val snickered. "So you *are* working for demons."

Payton buried his fingers in Doris's fur. "I don't know what you're talking about."

"Sure," Val said, his jaw fixed.

Twyla stepped closer to Payton. "Either you're working for the demon Mammon"—she paused for dramatic effect—"or he is working for you."

Payton clenched his hand around Doris's neck. The cat shrieked, then jumped free of his grasp.

"I don't do anyone's bidding," Payton spat.

"I take that as a yes," Val said dryly.

"No," Payton claimed. "She's skittish. It doesn't mean anything."

Val scoffed. "Oh, it speaks volumes."

"This is ridiculous. You're just trying to mess with my head," Payton ground out. He slid to the edge of the chair.

"How are you communicating with Mammon?" Val demanded.

"Oh, you know, telepathy, through the TV, summoning," Payton said sarcastically. He jumped up, then lunged at Val.

The sheriff darted backward. "I think that's it—you summoned him."

Twyla glanced around the room. "He would have had to create a portal." She walked the outer edges of the room, examining the walls and floor.

"I've been down here for a year—being held as a prisoner. I have no connections," Payton growled.

She searched the kitchen, then turned through a doorway that led to the bedroom. "What are you looking for?" Val asked.

"A pentagram. There must be one around here somewhere," she said. "It's a necessary part of any demon-summoning ceremony."

Val joined the search, peering behind pictures and moving furniture.

"Isn't it bad enough you have me locked up? Must you disturb my cell, too?" Payton asked with a sigh.

Twyla focused inward, letting her senses rule. She followed the hot, sickening vibrations that were coming to her. They led to the bedside table. She moved it aside, its legs scraping against the floor. Looking down, she saw a rough cut five-pointed star set within a circle etched into the floor. A dead rat was squished against the wall. She scrunched her face in disgust. "Found it."

Val came up behind her, glancing over her shoulder. "What does that mean?"

She breathed in his musky, smoky scent. God, he smelled good. She tried to shake that thought off. "It's a portal to the demonic world. Mammon, or whatever demon he summoned, probably visited Payton through this." In a whisper, she finished, "I think the rat was an offering."

Val glared at Payton. "Looks like you'll be getting new quarters."

Payton kicked at the cat. She quickly dashed out of the way before his foot struck. "You'll never find what you're searching for," he grunted.

"We will. Eventually." Val clasped Payton's arm above the elbow, then jerked him out of his chair and through the outer doorway. Twyla followed them down the hallway to another metal door. This one had traditional thick metal prison bars. Val opened it, practically shoving the vampire inside. "No more cushy accommodations."

Doris trailed them. She veered between the bars just as Val shut it with a *clink* and a *click*. The cat slunk off to hide behind a chair.

As they moved away, Val's arm brushed Twyla's shoulder. The slight contact reminded him of his desire to protect her. He slipped a hand to the small of her back, guiding her. "What should we do about that pentagram? Is there a way to get rid of it?"

"I'm not sure we want to do that. It might be useful. I think we should leave it for now. Let me confer with Nora and Luna."

"At least now we have more information to take to the Council," he said. "And we know what is driving the discord among the veaklings…Mammon."

On the drive back to the mansion, Val called in a to-go order to Poltergeist Pizza. "Ground beef and mushrooms, okay?" He angled his cell phone to the side to ask.

"Sure."

"Yes, good," he said into the phone, then ended the call. He glanced over at her. "Fifteen minutes."

It only took five to get there. After parking, they sat with the engine running. "Best pizza in town."

She laughed. "Only pizza in town."

"Don't interrupt the anticipation of my taste buds," he said as he turned on the radio.

She reached over to the dash to turn it off.

"Hey, that was my favorite song!"

"Since when? You hate country music." She sighed heavily. "Can we talk about it now?"

His brow furrowed. "What?"

"The missing demon. The star was in Payton's

chambers—either for him to go through or for a demon to come earth-side."

"Oh. You really want to talk about demons? I don't want to upset you."

"The pentagram was intact. So the demon most likely came through to do Payton's bidding. Don't you think?"

He checked the time on his phone. "Pizza is ready. I'll be right back." He slid from his Jeep, went inside, and bought the pizza. Part of him wanted to discuss what they'd discovered in Payton's cell. Twyla's witch family was an excellent source to tap when it came to demons. But a greater part of him wanted to shut her out. Maybe even send her to her mom's. Keeping her away from Mammon would mean she'd stay safe. At least that was what he hoped.

After he climbed in the Jeep, he handed her the red-and-white pizza box. "Careful. It's hot," he warned. The smell of dough, sauce, and meat filled the vehicle. His stomach flip-flopped. Man, he was hungry.

"So you think we have a demon on our hands, also?" she said. "Mammon could be anywhere in Terror."

"You don't let up, do you?" He'd forgotten that about her.

She rolled her eyes. "We have to deal with this thing."

"*I* have to deal with it. *You* need to stay out of it."

She clamped her mouth shut, clearly aggravated. When he glanced at her face, her eyes shot daggers at him. It was okay if she were angry at him, especially if it were the price he had to pay to protect her. He could handle that.

He turned into his driveway, cut the engine, and took the box back from her. "I think I could eat this by myself."

"You'd have to fight me for it." They both hopped out of the Jeep, then headed into the house.

Val grabbed a couple of sodas from the refrigerator, then set them on the kitchen counter. Twyla opened the lid of the box and picked up a slice, then sank her teeth into the melted cheese. She slid onto a barstool.

Grinning, Val shook his head. "Nothing like a bit of tension to increase one's appetite."

"Mmm," she moaned. "I love pizza."

"Some things are better now than, say…a hundred years ago, huh?"

She took another piece of pizza. "Uh-huh. Bread was the closest thing we had back then."

"Twyla," he said, then paused. He wanted to tell her that he'd like to give their relationship another try. "I…"

She tilted her head. "What?"

But he couldn't do it. Not when he'd been the one to fail the last time. No, maybe when this current problem was resolved, he'd revisit his feelings for Twyla. Certainly, he could keep them buried until then.

He studied the granite countertop with its black swirls and ruby-red flecks, sneaking glances at her while they ate. When they were done, he grabbed the empty pizza box, folded it in half as he walked across the kitchen, and placed it in the trash.

"So how do we find the demon?" Twyla asked, tipping up her soda to take a sip.

"We don't. Not until Mammon shows himself." He cleared his soda can, pitching it in the trash. "And then *I* need to be ready. Let's go to the weapons room."

He led the way past the dining room table to a short hall across from the living room. They passed a powder room before entering through double pocket doors. Inside, the walls were lined with weapons. Glass-topped cases displayed knives and guns, both old and new. After making his way over to a safe that was set into the wall, he spun the lock mechanism. He opened the heavy, thick door, then reached in to remove a knife from its cradle.

As soon as he touched it, it began to glow with iridescent white light. "This is what we need for demons. A talum. An ancient magical weapon." It was about a foot long, seeming as if it were made from some type of stone crystal. He strapped it into a special holster on his thigh.

"Luna would appreciate that. She's the weapons-oholic in our family." Twyla held up her hand, cupping her palms and allowing sparks of energy to dance from her fingertips. "For me, it's the old ways of magic."

"If it works, that's all that counts."

Val led the way into the living room. He was rounding a chair when a thundering noise came from the front entry. "What the—"

Abruptly, the right side of the double door came off its hinges. It was hurled into the short hallway, flying through the air and landing on the glass dining room table, smashing it into pieces. Thousands of shards shot out in every direction, bursting throughout the room like crystal stars. A sharp pain exploded in his thigh, but he ignored the piercing sting. Val's gaze cut to Twyla, praying she wasn't injured, too. Thankfully, she hadn't cleared the hallway and had been protected by the wall.

It took him a moment to fully process what had happened. He glanced back at the table. A lesser demon hovered above it. The demon was a giant, misshapen blob of gray. It seemed to try to find a shape—something like a creature with horns and beaked nose—only to change to a hideous dog-like form seconds later. As if it couldn't quite hold on to anything substantial.

Which it couldn't.

It wasn't the smartest of demons, but it was mean and powerful. It was also *not* Mammon. And that odor of rotten flesh... Val almost gagged as he forced himself to inhale a fortifying breath, knowing what he had to do.

Out of the corner of his eye, he saw Twyla peek around the corner. "Stay back," he shouted. Val shot forward, glass crunching beneath his footsteps. He launched at the demon as he brandished his talum. "Go back where you came from."

He brandished the talum in an arch. The beast moved, but not quickly enough. The tip of his blade nicked the thing. Black ooze splattered onto Val's shirt and arm. He didn't care, though. He just stayed his course as the demon retreated to the curved staircase. Val stepped on top of the fallen door just as Twyla hurried to the entry table off to his right. In her bare hands, balls of flame danced once again. But this time, she hurled one, then another, at the demon. It dodged the first fireball by flying upward, but the second hit its side.

Lowering to the ground, the demon gurgled almost unintelligible words. "Kill…must kill."

The lesser demon sprang forward, throwing its massive form at Val.

Yep, not too smart.

Val drove the talum deep into the middle of the demon's chest. Its gray form twitched and howled. It shrank like a deflating balloon, emitting a slurping sound like the one that came when sucking out the last drops of a near-empty child's beverage that came with a straw.

Fizzling down to an inky spot the size of a half-dollar, the demon vanished with a cracking *pop.*

Twyla placed a hand on the wall to steady herself. "Are you okay?" she asked, her breaths coming in hard exhales.

"Yes," he said in a thick voice. He wanted to throttle and kiss her at the same time. She hadn't remained hidden as he'd instructed. On the other hand, he was proud of how she'd handled herself, bravely and with focus.

He hobbled off the fallen door, then collapsed onto a barstool. A glass shard as long as his hand protruded from his thigh.

Her eyes widened, then her mouth pinched as her eyes focused on his injury. She ran over. "You're hurt." Reaching over the countertop near the sink, she grabbed a dry dishcloth, then folded it. She met Val's eyes. "Do you want to do it, or should I?"

"I will." He took the cloth from her, wrapped it around the shard, and tugged upward, hissing through a clenched jaw.

After he dropped the glass on the counter, she ripped an opening in his jeans to assess the injury better. Blood still gushed from the wound, making it difficult to judge how deep it was. She took the dishcloth from him, pressing down firmly on the gash.

"It will heal," he promised. "Give it a few minutes."

But that wasn't good enough for Twyla. He could see that in her determined expression.

"So much blood," she whispered. Settling a glowing hand over the wound, she shut her eyes. It seemed as if she was cauterizing the wound by willing it to close.

He watched her, intrigued at first. Then he gritted his teeth as a searing pain ran over his skin.

When she pulled away, only a faint scar remained on his leg. "It healed even faster that way."

She stood next to him, leaning slightly forward. His eyes caught and held hers. The aftermath of violence transformed into passion, swirling around them as if binding them together. She tipped into him, roughly covering his mouth with hers in a searing kiss. He met her thrusting tongue, answering her desperate hunger.

When she pulled back on a heavy sigh, he said, "We're okay. The demon is gone."

With her forehead pressed against his, she nodded. "Right. Right." Slowly, she stepped back.

Val watched her for signs of distress. There were none.

She squared her shoulders. "That *wasn't* Mammon."

"No." He shook his head. "A lesser demon is nothing but a minion."

"So, it seems Mammon has allowed others through the pentagram."

"Evidently. And we have no way of knowing how many or what sort of beasts we're dealing with…"

8

"I'm sorry about your table," Twyla said, glancing around the dining room at the bare metal frame.

He swept the last of the glass into a dustpan before dumping it in the trash. "I can have another one made."

She sensed anger in him, yet she didn't understand it. Was he upset with…her? She didn't know why he would be. She'd only done what he would have had their roles been reversed—helped fight off the beast. She wasn't as good as Luna when it came to fighting—her sister was fierce and a natural warrior—but what had Val wanted her to do? Hide like a damsel in distress while waiting for him to rescue her? That wasn't how McGuires were wired. She'd been raised to carry her own weight, including during battle.

"Now what?" she asked, trying to ignore his negative aura as best she could.

"We need to inform the Council of the latest developments. I wouldn't be surprised if it required a unified effort to drive the demons back to Hell where they belong."

"I'll help in any way I can," Twyla said, perching on the arm of the sofa.

"You're not a Council member. You should stay out of it."

"I'm already in it," she pointed out. "That happened when Ethan abducted me, then marked my door. Or maybe even earlier when I spelled the Ruin Coin to bind his powers."

"Even so, you're—"

"Not a Council member, I know. But my mother is. Find a way to bring me to the next Paranormal Council meeting."

"It's not that easy. There are rules to follow."

"Screw the rules," she said, her aggravation clear in her tone.

His jaw tensed. "Your mother shouldn't have even told you she is a Council member."

"It's difficult to keep secrets in our family."

He nodded. "I'll do what I can. But for now, we should get some rest."

"Yeah. Fighting demons can wear you out." She stretched, arching her head back and her chest out. "I'll see you in the morning." She walked to the staircase. Leisurely strolling up the stairs, she paused now and then to glance over her shoulder, feeling him watching her ascent. His eyes touched her with longing as if he didn't want to let her go.

Once at the top, she could no longer see him. She entered her suite. The room was elegant. A luxurious queen bed occupied most of the room. It was so high she needed to use the nearby stool to get in the bed. Two nightstands and an upright dresser made from cherry wood completed the furnishing, all quite different from her wrought-iron furniture and her bed with a gauze canopy and twinkling lights. And there wasn't a plant in sight.

She ducked through the double-pocket doors of the en-suite bathroom, staring at the Jacuzzi tub in the center with anticipation. A long, hot soak would feel wonderful. Off to the left was a walk-in shower complete with body jets. She bit her lip in indecision. Bath or shower?

With a happy sigh, she turned on the tub faucets and lit a tower candle on a stand next to a bowl of bath bombs. The candle was the same basil-and-mint scent Val used in his chambers. Inhaling the familiar fragrance, she dropped in a bomb with the same fragrance.

When the tub was full, she slipped off her clothes and secured her hair, then climbed in and turned on the jets. Her body immediately went limp as she soaked up the water's warmth.

Muscles relaxing, she closed her eyes. Soon, the bubbles and air flitting over her skin brought to mind the tenderness of Val's hands. The way he once skimmed his fingers over her body, teasing lightly over her skin, making her tingle with yearning. He was a big man, but he was a gentle and attentive lover. A moan escaped her lips as she recalled the times they'd spent together.

Abruptly, she sat up. She began to scrub her skin, trying to wash away her blossoming memories. Like the wisteria climbing her garden gate, they needed to be pruned and cut back with care or else they would choke out everything else.

And then maybe she could reseed the fertile ground in her heart that still loved Val.

*

Twyla tossed and turned in bed. Throwing back the covers, she dangled in that foggy murk between wakefulness and sleep. At the edges of her mind, a monarch butterfly fluttered over a camellia bush. It landed on a bright pink flower, then moved to the next, and the next. It flitted through the air, playing among the oak branches before finally settling on a fence post.

The sky was the deep blue of late afternoon, and the air hung moist and thick. It was summer, and there wasn't a breeze to be had. A massive, dark form hovered over her. She looked up to see a sinister black shadow of a beast. A demon.

Realizing the danger, the butterfly frantically beat its wings, trying to fly away. But the shadow formed arms and a head with a hooked beak. It swung one arm in an arc, snatching the butterfly in midair before crushing it in its fist.

With a gasp, Twyla sprang up in bed, her heart thudding in her chest and ears. The mattress dipped beneath her, the sheets feeling warm where she'd been resting. But the bed no longer seemed inviting. All she could see behind her eyelids was the demon chasing her, catching her, and killing her.

She slid off the mattress. Forgetting about the long drop to the floor, she stumbled forward. Luckily, she caught her balance. She reached for the bottled water on the nightstand, then took a long drink.

It was just a dream.

After she took a few deep breaths, her pulse began to calm. She closed her eyes, testing the images were gone, but the vile demon still lurked. Her pulse shot up again.

As she glanced at the clock on the nightstand, she started pacing. She'd only been asleep for forty-five minutes. Definitely not long enough to be up for the day.

For a little while, she sat in the chair, occasionally sipping at her water. Then she climbed back in bed, dragging the covers to her chin. An hour passed, but it felt far longer. And still, she was so tense and uneasy that she knew she wouldn't be able to sleep.

Perhaps a snack will help.

She padded downstairs, then searched the refrigerator.

Nose crinkling, she sighed. Val didn't stock much food she liked. She grabbed an apple before she closed the door.

As she ate, her gaze fell on what was left of the dining table. Val had been strong and fearless while fighting that demon. She'd seen glimpses of his dragon. It must have been frustrating not to be able to change due to the confines of his home.

Before she realized it, only the apple core remained. She tossed it in the garbage.

With her foot on the first step of the staircase, she hesitated, a tightness coiling in her stomach. She shifted her gaze to Val's bedroom door. He represented calm, comfort, and security. Perhaps, he'd even help her achieve freedom from her nightmare.

Without contemplating the consequences, she changed course. She made her way toward his bedroom. The door was slightly propped open, and she peered in. She could make out his shape occupying the right side of the king-sized bed. She slowly tiptoed to the left side, slipped beneath the covers, and curled up, facing away from him. Closing her eyes, she immediately fell into a peaceful sleep.

Val was a light sleeper. When the bed dipped, he tensed and opened his eyes. Twyla's fragrance drifted into his nostrils. His body reacted swiftly, and he tightened his jaw.

Judging from the way she hugged the opposite edge of the bed, she didn't hunger for the same thing he did. He let out a slow, silent breath.

Suddenly, a torturous night seemed to be in his future. But knowing Twyla as he did, the demon incident had finally caught up with her and she hadn't been able to sleep. But by the sounds of her even breathing, that wasn't the case any longer.

He slipped his hands into his hair, cradling his head as he stared at the black ceiling. *Go back to sleep*, he urged his dragon.

Concentrating on the sounds outside—the wind and the tree scraping against the house from the gusts—*he needed to trim those branches*—the pitter-patter of an animal scurrying across leaves, the distant whir of an airplane passing overhead—he shut his eyes, pretending Twyla wasn't sleeping in his bed. When that didn't work, he resorted to another tactic, recounting all the times they'd slept together. And somehow, he wasn't sure why, he'd drifted off.

Hours later, he awoke to someone shaking his arm. "Val, wake up."

He jumped. When he saw it was Twyla, he stretched. "You're in my bed," he stated.

"I had a bad dream," she said as if that explained everything. "It's ten o'clock. We need to get started."

"Get started on what?" he asked groggily, pushing to his elbows and meeting her eyes.

"Talking to the Council. You need to call a meeting."

"Oh. That." He dropped back on the pillow.

"Time's a-wastin'."

"Most paranormals aren't even awake yet."

She sat up. Tucking her legs beneath her, she pushed her ink-black hair over her shoulders. In a strappy coral-colored tank top that read *Good Vibes Only* with a butterfly-and-flower print and little shorts that showed every inch of her shapely legs, she was lovely. "Do you have a plan?"

He remembered now that Twyla was much too perky in the morning. She usually hit the ground running with her coffee in one hand while whistling a tune.

"No…" He groaned. "I have to wake up first."

She swung her feet to the floor. "Okay. Then get up, and let's go. I'll put the coffee on." She rose, winked, then strolled out the door.

Val rolled onto his side, but couldn't help his grin. He'd missed having her around.

After donning a shirt and pants, he went downstairs and came up behind her in the kitchen. She'd already poured two cups of coffee, and was in the process of doctoring hers with cream and sugar. Her hair was split into two segments, each pulled to the front and draped over each shoulder like a shawl. The monarch butterfly tattoo on the back of her neck was left exposed. He hadn't seen it in an extremely long time…

He bent to kiss the butterfly, feeling her shiver beneath his lips. Then he pressed another kiss higher on her neck, then her ear. "Thank you for making coffee," he whispered, his voice still heavy with sleep.

"You're welcome."

She turned, handing him a mug. He eased back to give her some room. Sipping his coffee, he gazed over the rim as she smiled at him. Coffee had never tasted so good.

"I had an idea to draw Mammon out. Why not use me as bait?" she said, then sank her upper teeth into her lower lip. She pinned her hopeful brown eyes on his face.

"What? No." Her foolish idea had him instantly wide awake. There was no way he'd use her to draw out the demon.

"Payton wants me to remove the Ruin Coin, right? So we tell him that's exactly what I will do, and I'm sure Mammon will hear as well."

"And why would he believe you'd do that?

She shrugged. "So he would leave me alone. So I wouldn't be a pawn in the middle of law enforcement work. I don't know. Pick a reason he'd latch on to."

"No, I'll come up with another plan." Val walked away from her, drinking his coffee. The hot liquid wasn't near as firey as the fear in his gut. He wouldn't do anything that would put her in danger.

As if reading his mind, she said, "You can be right nearby to jump in if Mammon shows up, then confront him if needed."

"Any plan with you in the middle of it is *not* a good one. Remind me why you have to be the bait…"

"Because I'm the one who put the hex on the Ruin Coin. So only I can take it off," she said.

"Damn it. I don't like it." His fists opened, then closed.

"I trust you to keep me safe." She turned to refill her cup.

He came to her, his demeanor softening as he set his cup on the counter and encircled her in his arms. "I will always keep you safe." His lips brushed over hers.

"I know." She rested against his chest for a long minute. "Do you want something to eat?" she asked.

He snickered. *Um, yes. You.* "Yes. But I'll fix it." He got the necessary ingredients from the fridge. "I'm guessing you didn't sleep well?"

"Not at first," she admitted.

He nodded. "Can I fix you something, too?"

"Whatever you're having is fine."

"Good. Lox and caviar, it is."

"What?" she squealed. Then her eyes met his, and she smiled. "Oh. You're teasing."

He grinned. "That happens occasionally." He set the ingredients on the counter. "Now, how about an omelet?"

"That sounds delicious." She nodded eagerly. "Thank you."

"You just sit and relax," he said as he started cooking.

She went around to the bar side of the counter, then took a seat. He was sorry he'd suggested it because of how much farther away it put her. But they chatted about her garden while he prepared their meal. Twenty minutes later, he set their plates and silverware on the counter.

Thankfully, the omelet looked like it had turned out perfectly—he tended to get miffed when it didn't. "Dig in."

She took a bite, then groaned. "Heaven."

He laughed. "I'm not sure it's that good, but thanks." He ate a forkful. "Okay, it is."

She shook her head, smiling. Having breakfast with her again felt so right. It was like old times when it had been good between them. Before he'd messed it up by getting too serious about his job…

The chemistry between them flared whenever he allowed it to. Could she ever give him another chance?

*

It was drizzling when he shifted into his dragon form to fly to Diego's Bike Shop where the Council meeting was to be held. Val could come and go less conspicuously in that shape since he wouldn't have to park his Jeep in public. That eliminated any concern of drawing suspicion if someone saw the vehicle.

Twyla hiked up her black trench coat as she climbed up his arm, then settled onto his back. Her soft steps tickled. He'd taken her home earlier that afternoon so she could tend her plants, change clothes, and check on some things, including brushing up on her knowledge of and spells about demons, so they'd left from her house.

He flew around the outskirts of town. Diego's place was on the southeastern side. When they reached it, he came in low and landed in the rear parking lot.

Twyla climbed down, shaking the rain off her hair and clothes. "You owe me a hot shower when we get home," she complained as he shifted back into his human form.

He chuckled. "My hot water heater is on demand, so no problem."

Val opened the side door to the bike shop for her to enter. They walked to the rear of the building into a lounge. It looked like they were the last to arrive. Everyone was seated except for Nora. Eight sets of eyes focused on them as they entered.

"What is she doing here?" Omar asked in his smooth, singsong voice.

Val's gaze shot to Nora. When he'd filled her in on the latest events, she had agreed Twyla could attend.

Omar turned to Nora. "These are closed meetings— even to family."

"Calm down, reaper," Nora said, meeting his concerned gaze with a wink. "The sheriff will explain."

"Omar is right, y'all," Simon said in his southern drawl. "We have rules we must abide by."

"Wait." Val held up his hand. "Twyla is at the center of the problem. Payton blames her for the Ruin Coin. And he's found a way to call up a demon."

Twyla loudly cleared her throat. "*Demons*. Plural."

Diego slid to the edge of his seat. "*Mierda*, how many?"

"We're not sure. But one less after last night," Val said.

"Jesus. We can't allow them to get comfy, or we'll never get rid of them." Diego ran a hand over his short, neatly trimmed beard. "Years ago, I had a bad run-in with demons before I left Cuba. It's not an easy fix."

"I understand that," Val said. "Maybe we'll get lucky and only have to deal with Mammon."

Diego grimaced. "Man, I shouldn't have given up smoking."

"Why's that?" Twyla asked, tilting her head curiously.

"Because if I'm gonna die, it should be from something I enjoy and not from some ugly-butt stink bomb."

Sissy LaFleur laughed, her champagne-colored wings ruffling with the movement. "They do reek. But you're not going to die, you crazy Cuban."

Diego's talk of death struck a chord in Val. He should have taken Twyla in his arms last night and made love to her until the wee hours of the morning. He'd been foolish to think he could ignore what he felt for her. He hadn't been able to commit when she'd wanted him to before—when she'd pressured him about having children someday, about giving up his job, and about making a life together. But now, suddenly, he wanted her more than anything else.

Val knew their lighthearted banter was a ploy to thumb their noses at fate. They all knew the damage a demon could do; it was just easier not to admit it.

Diego tossed his head back with a dismissive wolf growl.

"There must be a way to flush them out," Nora said.

"There is." Nathaniel stood, then trudged over to stand beside Val. His eyes were hard, filled with hunting experience.

"Yes. But I can't say I like it." Val watched Nate's expression, then shifted his gaze to Twyla to see if they were on the same page. She gave a little nod. "We use bait," he finally said.

Nate nodded. "Exactly what I was thinking."

"What kind of bait?" Diego inquired.

"The same bait Ethan used to begin with…Twyla," Val announced, side-eyeing Twyla apprehensively.

A rumble of voices ran through the room as the group reacted to his words. He wished he could think of another way to draw the demons out, but he hadn't been able to. He'd chided himself for his stupidity at not coming up with another solution. But, as Diego had expressed, once the demons settled in, they were damned hard to get rid of. And Val couldn't allow them to stay. He had a duty to the town. Val intended to fight the beasts off while protecting Twyla in the process, just as he'd done last night.

"Now wait a minute," Nora spoke up. "You didn't mention anything about using my daughter as bait when we spoke earlier."

"I hadn't agreed to Twyla's plan then."

"Twyla's plan?" Nora glared at her daughter.

Val nodded. "It's not my decision to make. It's up to the Council…and Twyla." Val met each member's gaze. "We need a unified front. Who's ready to stand with me in this fight?"

Justin Smith raised a fist. "I am," he pledged.

Val admired his courage. But the ex-Green Beret was the one person he didn't need on his team this time. The man's humanity made him extremely vulnerable. But showing his respect, Val nodded at the guy anyway. "Okay."

"I'm in," Diego said.

"Me too," Sissy added.

"This is my daughter you're talking about. You aren't going anywhere without me," Nora chimed in, her voice louder than the rest as she pulled her shoulders back.

Every being in the room raised a hand in agreement.

"Good," Diego said. "Then we're the magnificent nine."

Twyla cleared her throat. "Ten."

"Ten?" Sissy protested.

"Sure. You better be counting me in," Twyla said.

"She's right," Diego pointed out. He said it seriously, yet with his usual smart-ass grin.

"Um, thanks," Val said, waiting for everyone to settle down again. Tamping down the uneasy feeling in his stomach, he pressed on. "So this is what I propose…"

10

Twyla hadn't said much throughout the meeting. She was an outsider, so she felt she should keep quiet. Plus, she trusted Val to look out for her best interests. At least, that was what she had told herself going in. But the nervous tension inside her grew more as the meeting continued. She wasn't sure how much longer she could hold it in.

"Payton wants Twyla to remove the spell on the holding collar," Val explained. "We will tell him she'll do it if he sends the demons back to Hell."

"Will he believe she will, though?" Nora asked.

"Oh, yes. He wants it so badly that I think he'll jump at any morsel we give him," Val said.

"I will convince him," Twyla added.

"Besides, he probably doesn't truly care for dealing with the demons. After all, they are more powerful than him," Sissy said.

Val nodded. "But can we do this in a location other than his cell? I'd like to move him to a larger location.

One we can all move around freely in. Plus, one with enough room to allow me to change into my dragon should the need arise."

"I can handle that," Nora said. "I'll create another pentagram."

Val folded his arms over his chest. "Okay, good. I think we should do it at Raven's Roost. It's abandoned, and it's well away from the main part of town."

"Excellent," Nate agreed.

"So, what is it you want us to do?" Diego asked.

"Be there in force," Val said, "and be prepared to use whatever magical powers you possess."

"And me? What is the bait's job?" Twyla hated the crack in her voice.

Val stood to his full height, faced her, and placed his hands on her shoulders. "We will rehearse exactly what you will say. You are our voice, and we are your armed guards. No harm will come to you." He gazed deeply into her eyes. "I promise."

Swallowing hard, Twyla nodded once. She believed in him. Trusted him. His voice was confident and sure. And if he would just put his arms around her, she'd feel even safer. But that would surely compromise his leadership during the mission.

"All right, we're set. Meet us there tomorrow evening at ten o'clock sharp," Val stepped back so the other members could leave first.

Val looked over at Twyla's mother. "Nora, I want Twyla to arrive with you," he said. "I don't think she should be alone until we've sent those demons back. She can stay with me until late tomorrow when I leave for the jail. But after that—"

"Of course she will go with me," Nora said, flipping the dark ends of her hair over her shoulder. "I've been watching after her for her entire life. I would have it no other way."

Seeming satisfied, Val placed his hand on the small of Twyla's back, the warmth of his touch comforting. "Ready to go?"

"Oh yeah." She grabbed her coat from the back of the chair.

By then, everyone except Diego had left. He walked them out, then locked the door behind them. "You have some beautiful bikes in there. When we're finished with all this drama, I'll have to stop in to take a look."

"Humph. You need to drop in to buy," Diego said, pausing on the outside staircase that led to his apartment above the shop.

Val laughed. "That, too."

"Hey, then you can join our riding group. We go for a tour every Saturday."

Twyla wondered about that group. She'd seen them driving around. They did a lot of charity work, even down south in Minneapolis.

"Okay." Val gave him a fist bump before guiding her to the parking lot behind the building. The rain had stopped, but the air was still thick with moisture.

On the ride home, she felt so tired she rested against the smooth, rippling scales of Val's back, wrapping her arms as far as she could around his dragon's thick neck. He was surprisingly warm, perhaps from all the heat he stored inside himself. She sighed, a peacefulness rinsing away all her earlier doubt. Closing her eyes, she held on tight.

Too soon, he landed back at the mansion. Once she dismounted and he'd shifted back, he slipped his hand in hers and they walked inside.

"I feel like Guinevere and her knight Lancelot. I shouldn't be telling you this because I'm sure it will go to your head, but there's something romantic about dragons. I hadn't thought about it…until I flew with you."

"Romantic, hmm?" He stopped along the walkway, shifting her in his arms. "Hold that thought." He kissed her with all the warmth and desire tugging at his heart. "I don't want to pretend I don't want to hold you, or I don't care about you any longer. Or that I don't want you in my life."

She raised a brow. "That sounds like a lot of negatives."

"Can we try again? Just see where it leads us?" he asked, pressing his lips to her forehead.

"I'd like that," she said with a smile.

He kissed her, lifting her feet off the ground and twirling her around. When he set her down, she laughed and asked, "What are you doing?"

"Rewinding the clock."

"Oh," she said, her voice a wispy sigh as she leaned into him.

Draping an arm around her shoulders, he guided her into the kitchen. He'd had a crew out this morning to fix the broken door the demon had knocked off its hinges. It was temporary because the matching wood had to be special ordered. He paused at the refrigerator. "Would you like some ice cream?"

"Sure."

He dished out some blackjack cherry ice cream, then drizzled chocolate syrup over the top the way he knew she liked it. Twyla closed the syrup cap with her finger, getting chocolate on it. She was about to wipe it off, but he grabbed her hand and licked the syrup away.

A caress of sensations—warm, familiar, and right— melted through him. He cupped her cheek with his hand, searching her eyes. "Sleep with me tonight. I want to make love to you."

She nestled her face into his palm. When she kissed a spot near his thumb, he could feel the steady throb of his pulse against her lips. "I want that, too."

He picked up the two bowls of ice cream. "Will you get the spoons?" he asked over his shoulder. "We'll have this in bed." He shot her a wink. Pausing at the end of the counter, he waited for her to grab two spoons from a drawer. Together, they walked past the broken table—an eerie reminder of the perils they had yet to face—and into his bedroom.

Tomorrow. They'd deal with what they had to tomorrow. Tonight was only about them.

11

Twyla woke to the sounds of birds singing outside. She was tucked under Val's arm, resting her head on his shoulder. "I've missed this," she admitted.

"Yeah. Me too."

She closed her eyes, feeling his heartbeat against her cheek. Her stomach growled, and she laughed. "I guess I worked up an appetite."

After a deep kiss, he untangled himself from her body, then rose from the bed. "I'll get us some bagels and coffee."

She stretched. "Let's eat on the porch." After he nodded, she got out of bed, wrapped the sheet around her like a toga, and followed him to the kitchen.

"Go on out. I'll bring you breakfast," he said, gesturing toward the glass double doors that opened onto a veranda running the length of the house.

After pressing a kiss to his lips, she did as he'd suggested. She sat in an Adirondack chair overlooking the backyard. A beautiful rose garden was in full bloom, and the scent of the flowers floated toward her on the slight morning breeze. As she watched the birds attack the feeder, Val came through the door. He carried a tray with coffee, toasted cinnamon bagels, and strawberries. Once he set it on a small table, he took the other seat.

"Thank you," she said. "How perfect."

"You're welcome."

They ate while enjoying the fresh air. She couldn't believe the way things had turned around for her and Val. Thinking of the night they'd just shared, she sighed. She wasn't in a hurry to test their relationship. Instead, she intended to relish the moment. Perhaps she'd pushed him too hard last time, been too adamant and impatient. She wished she could say she had changed and mellowed, but that wasn't the case. If anything, she was more persistent. She often felt that life was passing her by.

At the same time, resentment niggled at her. When she'd agreed to place the spell on Payton's Ruin Coin, she hadn't thought it would end in on someone terrorizing her because of it. She shivered, recalling the lesser demon and wondering just how much Payton could accomplish from the confines of his cell. Of course, it helped him to have minions to do his bidding.

She wasn't the bravest witch in the world. The brave ones were her sword-wielding sisters Luna and Solis. They were both fierce, stubborn, and plain awesome. She sighed. Not her. She was a nurturer who liked nature—not fighting.

"Are you cold?" Val asked.

Her brow pinched. "No."

He didn't seem convinced. "I saw you shiver. I can get you a blanket."

"It's not the temperature. I was thinking of the demons. But I'm all right."

He lifted his chin and jerked his head, inviting her over. "Come sit on my lap."

He didn't have to ask twice. In three steps, she was beside him. He tugged her down, catching her in his arms. She rested her head against his neck and shoulder, sinking into him.

"That's much better." He smiled down at her.

She snuggled against his warm body. They sat that way for a while, cuddling. Finally, he shifted her until he could see her face.

"We need to discuss this evening. When you arrive, I want you to stay close to your mother. No heroics, understand?"

She pursed her lips. "I hear ya."

"Hearing me and doing what I suggest isn't the same thing," he pointed out.

"They are not suggestions—they're orders. And in case you haven't noticed, I can make up my own mind."

"Oh, believe me, I've noticed. It's why I'm getting prematurely gray." He ran a hand through his coffee-brown hair.

With mock interest, she scrutinized him. "There isn't any gray."

"If tonight's plan fails, you'll find a shock of white, I promise." He hesitated. "Seriously, Twyla, I worry about you. I don't know what I'd do if anything happened to you."

She shifted in his lap, brushed her mouth over his lips, then brushed their noses together. "It won't."

"Nora will bring you to the meeting place. My first responsibility will be to keep Payton Grey confined. Since we're going to meet you outside his cell, that should get him hyped up. I'm counting on his inflated ego. He'll think he can beat us by calling in the demons he's summoned. Then Nora will send the beasts through the pentagram and back to where they belong. Any suggestions?"

"What about Payton?"

"We place a new spell on him. Maybe turn him into a frog," he said with a laugh.

"Hey, I happen to like frogs," she teased. "They play an important role in the ecosystem by eating insects."

"Of course they do." He pushed her back a bit, finger-combing her silky hair. Almost purring, she leaned into his touch. It felt so good. "I could do this all day," he said. "But we should get ready."

She rose from his lap. Once he stood, he began to pick up the dishes. She hurried to help. As they went inside, she wanted to ask if he genuinely thought they could pull off this plan. Instead, she pressed her lips together. He would be honest with her—that much she knew. She just wasn't quite sure if she was ready for the truth.

Val's boots scraped against the cobblestone drive as he walked to the porch of the sheriff's office. His spine straightened when he saw the open entrance. He stalked inside. "What's the door to the back doing open?" he asked Trevor.

Trevor dropped his feet off the desk with a quick, "Gotta go," into his cell phone. To Val, he said, "I don't know. I guess the latch didn't catch."

Val didn't like the sound of that. His gut tensed. The doors were always kept locked. He hurried outside. Folding his arms across his chest, he stood on the porch and surveyed the area. The evening sky was clear and the moon shone bright, making it easy to distinguish the road, buildings, and their neighbors. He glanced around. Nothing seemed out of place, so headed back in.

It had been a pleasant day. He'd spent the morning with Twyla before dropping her off at Beauty & Beast at lunchtime. Nora had fixed him a plate of graveyard greens to go. There had been so much he had brought a to-go box back for Trevor.

He slid the container of leftovers, along with a fork, onto the desk. "Courtesy of Nora."

Trevor opened the box, grinned, and dug in. "Thanks," he said between bites.

"It's quiet. Too quiet." Val stood at the window, gazing out. The jail was located in the northwestern corner of town. Close enough to walk to Nevermore Lane to pick up a pizza or coffee, but set back away from the everyday foot traffic. Now was one of those times he was glad for its remote location.

Val went outside again, scanned up and down the street, then went back in and firmly shut the door behind him. Propping a hip on Trevor's desk so he'd be close enough to speak quietly, he explained the plan. Vampires had excellent hearing, but Val was reasonably sure the underground distance and rock created a buffer.

"Do you want me to come with?" Trevor asked, leaning his chair back and rocking it a few times.

"If you'd like. It's always good to have a backup."

"I'd be glad to. Except for Payton, things have been boring lately."

"Nothing wrong with boring." Val chuckled.

"Says the sheriff who's never home."

Val checked his watch. "Let's give ourselves a little extra time and head down." He unlocked the weapons cabinet, then removed a vial of holy water, a gun with silver bullets, and a silver sword. He passed the latter to Trevor—standard weapon used against a traditional vampire. Val's talum was already strapped to his leg.

Taking a deep breath, Val opened the door to the hallway leading to the cells reserved for supernaturals with abilities that made escape a possibility. The motion-sensor lights came on as they traveled through the passageway.

Val approached the cell he'd locked Payton in. He looked inside. It was empty.

"Payton," he said, his voice a fiery growl. "Shit. I can't believe this." He slammed his palm against the metal bars. They caved under pressure, creating a giant hand-sized imprint.

"The door is still locked from the outside," Trevor noted. "How in the world did he escape?"

"They could have locked it from the outside when they left. Perhaps to make some stupid point. But, otherwise, I don't know. He damn sure didn't trace with that Ruin Coin on. He had to have had help."

"By who?"

"My bet is on the demons."

Trevor's face twisted in disgust. "Great. I haven't had a putrid mud bath in ages," he said with a shudder.

"It's not the mud I'm worried about. Some spew poison." Val tromped to the first-class cell Payton had occupied until they'd discovered the pentagram. He entered, then checked the marking. Upon closer inspection, he noticed a smear of shiny black slime covering one edge of the symbol. He wasn't sure if it were because of something he'd read or sheer instinct, but he poured a bit of the holy water over the five-point star. The water bubbled and sputtered as if it were in a hot frying pan.

"What are you doing?" Trevor whispered, glancing between the star and Val.

Val lifted a shoulder. "It works on veakling vampires and some demons, so I thought it might cleanse the star. Maybe make it so nothing more could enter or exit."

"It will eventually evaporate," Trevor pointed out.

"Yes. It won't last long, but it might buy us some time." Val hurried toward the door.

Trevor followed him. "You don't think they went through the star, do you?"

"No. Only a demon would willingly use the star. I made a mistake by not getting rid of it," he said, fisting his hand. "We need to meet with the others to warn them. At some point, Payton will search out Twyla to get her to remove the Ruin Coin. Who knows what else he'll try?"

Val swiftly led the way out. Twyla and the group would be expecting Payton to be restrained by Val when they arrived. But that wouldn't be the case. And the only thing Payton couldn't do was trace… Free and without hindrance, the veakling would be a strong and brutal opponent.

Val needed to warn Twyla. He needed to be with her to protect her. And he needed to be there ten minutes ago.

Raven's Roost was a large, abandoned building made of ancient stone. At ten o'clock at night, it loomed dark and foreboding behind her. Twyla watched as her mother conjured a firestone, then set it in the middle of the lawn. It emitted enough light so the members of the Paranormal Council could see one another and the surrounding lawn.

Her mother's energy simmered just below the surface as she paced. Her hand opened and closed over the hilt of the sword she had strapped to her hip. A childhood memory surfaced at the movement, one Twyla had long forgotten. Nora had pushed her four children behind her while she faced off with a malevolent jinn who had been set on taking two of her kids. Twyla couldn't remember why. She only recalled her fear as the jinn tried to snatch at Luna. But talk about the wrath of a mama bear protecting her cubs. There was nothing left of the jinn when her mother had finished brandishing her sword and working her magic.

Twyla touched her sword. She wasn't sure she could ever fight like that. Her power was all in her magic, which came from within.

"What's taking them so long?" Nora asked.

Her mother's question pulled Twyla out of her thoughts. Her gaze swept the group. They were a motley crew. She hurried toward the steps where they had gathered.

Sissy and Omar leaned against the gray flagstone pillars that supported the building's portico. They were a contradiction in every way. Her fair complexion and blond hair appeared frail and delicate compared to his bronzed Middle Eastern skin. They were a brilliant example of the idiom, *You can't judge a book by its cover*. The angel could often be sassy and fierce, while the reaper was quiet and thoughtful.

Diego lounged on his bike, leaning back with his elbow propped on the seat as if he didn't have a care in the world. Justin seemed to be trying to get some point across to him with big hand gestures and a fist slamming against his palm.

Annabelle flitted between the group members, her fairy wings moving so quickly they were challenging to see with the naked eye. She didn't join in, but held herself apart. Perhaps it was her princess status that separated her from the rest; Twyla wasn't sure.

Nate sat on the steps next to Simon. Twyla dropped down beside them, resting her elbows on her knees with her chin on the heels of her palms.

"Come on. Let's get this over with," Nate mumbled. "I'd like to get home to my wife."

"How is Camille?" Simon asked.

"Great." Nate hesitated, then an uncertain laugh rumbled out of him. "We just found out she's expecting. I'm going to be a papa. Can you believe that?"

Everyone's attention snapped to Nate, many with wide eyes and dropped jaws.

"What? Well, I guess it's clear who's *not* your best friend seeing as I was left in the dark," Diego grumbled, straightening from his bike. "Congrats, man." He reached out to shake Nate's hand with a lazy smile.

"Thanks. We haven't told anyone else yet."

In the middle of the subsequent round of congratulations, Twyla's phone chimed. It was Val. She turned her back on the group so she could hear him better.

"Payton escaped," were the first words he said.

"What?" It felt as if the wind had been knocked out of her. "You've got to be kidding me."

Val sounded harsh and distraught. "It may take him some time to find you, but I have no doubt he will. On second thought, there's no way telling how long he's been free."

Someone commented in the background, but she couldn't quite hear it. "No more than an hour or so, according to Trevor. I'm heading to you now."

She nodded, even though he couldn't see her. "All right. I'll see you in a bit."

Everyone fell silent. All eyes were on her as she spun around. "Payton escaped," she said, allowing her gaze to sweep the darkness beyond the light of the firestone. *It wouldn't take an hour to get here from the police station.*

"Holy headlights," Diego said, slapping his palm down on the bike's saddlebag.

"Yeah. We figured we'd have to fight them anyway, right?" Twyla asked with a resigned shrug. She went for a blasé tone to keep the group calm. "Val is on his way."

"Payton will come after Twyla first," Nora said. "He'll want to get that Ruin Coin off."

The snap of branches sounded, followed by a loud scoffing noise. It came from across the lawn. Then Payton's haughty laugh rolled over the group. "You're so smart, Nora."

Almost in unison, the Paranormal Council closed ranks in front of Twyla.

Payton halted just within the circle of light. "Quite an

impressive group you have here, Twyla. But Nathaniel?" He clucked his tongue against his teeth. "A bounty hunter? You all let just about anyone in, don't you?"

He was staring straight at her, his dark eyes seeming so confident, so sure. If there were demons with him, she couldn't see them. But would he be this haughty without them?

"Let's even the odds a bit, shall we?" Payton said.

A movement to the right caught her eye. A disgusting dark form slid from the shadows. It had a serpent head with snake-like appendages attached to an upright body. A second later, another demon flanked Payton's left side. This one had cloven feet and the hindquarters of an animal—a cow or deer came to mind. Its head resembled that of a grotesque, disfigured goat. Slowly, a third shadowy figure showed itself behind goaty-goat. It reminded her of a slug—black, oily, and creepy.

Nora held court front and center of the group. She glanced from side to side, warning, "Take care. They aren't confined to the earthly rules of gravity and space. That one"—she directed her sword to the right—"is poisonous if it strikes you." Pointing to the left, she said, "And this gorgeous fellow, Mammon, guard your thoughts with him. He'll use them against you. He feeds on fear and greed. And slime-ball in the back, he'll latch on like a leech and suck the breath right out of you."

"Humph, you know your stuff, witch," Payton murmured.

Lightning fast, Nate traced within a few feet of Payton. "Give us a few minutes to dispatch these demons, and we'll have you back in jail in no time."

Payton peeled his lips back, showing his fangs, then gave another wicked laugh, ignoring Nate with an outward show of pleasure. "Twyla, simply undo the spell on the Ruin Coin, and I'll be on my way. No harm done."

She crossed her arms. "That's up to the Council."

"Ah, the *Council*." Payton gritted his teeth, fisting his hands. "The damned Council that has kept me locked up for an infernal year!" With his rising anger, the three figures stepped forward. Payton raised a hand to stop them. "Not yet."

He twisted to peer at the trio of demons. "Bring me the witch, Mammon, and the cobine will be yours," he growled.

"What would cobine be worth to demons?" Nate asked.

Payton shrugged. "It seems the cobine allows them to solidify their form for a short period. Who knew?"

Mammon's eyes shone with hunger. "Mine," he muttered in a guttural, almost unintelligible voice. "Kill."

With a sweep of his arm, Mammon sought to thrust Nate out of his way. Anticipating the blow, Nate jumped into the air, flipping and rotating as he went. He landed several feet away, out of Mammon's reach. "Missed me, demon."

Twyla felt guilty as the Paranormal Council prepared to fight for her. She stepped forward, advancing on Payton. With every stride, she pooled more and more of her magical power. The arcane force welled in her core and funneled along her arms, gathering and sparking blue light in her hands. Driven by her anger, she intended to strike first, but she was well aware of how unpredictable her magic could be.

Her focus intensified. So much so it took several seconds for her to realize her mother was speaking to her. "Twyla, stop. Let the Council handle this."

"No. Payton has made this my battle," she threw over her shoulder. "They can fight him if they want, but I won't stand helplessly by."

The lesser demon sprang from the left, lunging at her. She unleashed her full power without restraint. It annihilated the demon into a rain of black goo, some of which landed on Diego's arm.

"Oh, geez," he said as he flicked the glob off his leather

jacket with the tip of his sword.

Twyla nodded as her confidence swelled. *There. I can control my powers.* She glanced around. Swords had been drawn. Diego and Nate were engaged with the slithery demon while Sissy, Annabelle, and Omar fought Mammon.

Twyla met her mother's gaze. "I did it," Twyla said, somewhat amazed but proud of herself.

Nora came up beside her. "Well done, my child. Well done."

"Thank you," Twyla said, appreciative of her mother's rare praise. "Now, what do we do about Payton?" She approached the vampire while touching the red stone at her neck, drawing from its energy.

"Very impressive, my dear. All that vitality in the palm of your hand," Payton said. "May I touch it?"

"Not if you want to keep your fingers," Twyla coolly remarked.

Above them, two dragons circled. "Val and Trevor," Twyla said, looking up. Val's glowing silver-blue scales and powerful form was magnificent in flight. Trevor radiated hues of gold and red.

The dragons split, each joining a fight against a demon. It was like an air attack supporting the ground forces. The dragons took fireball shots, just missing. The tricky part, she imagined, was not to strike any of the Council members.

Annabelle raised her sword, lunging at the slithery one and cutting away a snake-like body part. Slithery spun around, striking her in the shoulder. She fell back with a scream. Nora jumped in. She swung her sword, stabbing the demon in the chest. It stumbled backward, shocked, then disintegrated.

A firm hand grabbed hold of Twyla, spinning her into a hard form. Payton had taken advantage of her distraction. He tightened his arm around her middle. "Remove the spell on the Ruin Coin," he ordered.

"No." She twisted, hoping to escape. Pain stabbed in her head. At first, she didn't know what was happening. Payton wasn't touching her head. Fear hit her in the chest, shooting through her. Images of being trapped, of being underground, rushed through her. He squeezed her harder. She couldn't breathe.

A few yards away, Sissy struck Mammon in the arm with her sword. But the demon was focused on Twyla. Nora ran over to join Sissy. "Control your thoughts, Twyla. It's Mammon."

No air. No air. She was aware of a dragon flying overhead. Omar ordered everyone to step back. There was a burst of flames.

A dragon rained fire down, striking the demon. Mammon opened his mouth, but before anything came out, the demon melted and disappeared. A curse split the air like a sonic boom.

Twyla jerked against Payton's grip. Her ribs expanded with a huge breath. She could breathe. It wasn't Payton who had played on her fearful thoughts of being trapped. It had been Mammon. She inhaled deeply.

Val landed, shifting into his human form. He looked magnificent. She felt Payton's stance change, so she took advantage, throwing her arms up and outward in a circular motion as she thrust her body away from him.

He tried to grab her again, but failed.

"They're gone," Twyla said in a rush.

"Back to the hellhole they came from," Nora added.

Val rushed over, pulled her to him, and ran a hand along her arm. "Are you okay?" he asked.

"Never better." She smiled enthusiastically, then kissed him.

"Aw, isn't that sweet?" Payton crooned. "Really, guys, get a cave or something. Isn't that where antediluvian dragons live?"

"Ooh, the vampire knows big words. It's all that reading he does in his cell. Which he's going right back to," Val said.

Payton's face contorted as if just now realizing he no longer had his demon support group. He retreated several steps, turned, and ran.

Val released her to pursue Payton. Since the veakling couldn't trace, he was no match for Val's powerful strides. Within moments, he caught up with Payton.

The vampire flung his arms out, trying to escape. Val hauled his fist back, slamming it into Payton's nose. "That's for daring to lay a hand on Twyla."

Payton stumbled backward, blood oozing down his face.

Payton ran his tongue over the wound, catching the blood on his tongue and drawing it into his mouth. He smiled. "Mmm."

"If it were up to me…" Val said, his mouth tightening, but he didn't finish. Grabbing Payton's arm, he roughly escorted him away from the group as they came together on the lawn.

The veakling laughed. "This was the best entertainment I've had in a year."

Trevor followed behind them without saying a word. She hadn't noticed he'd shifted into his human form. Then again, she'd been busy.

"Let's lock him up," Val called over his shoulder to Trevor.

"Be glad to." Trevor came up alongside the vampire. He snapped a handcuff on Payton's wrist, then linked the other to himself.

"I'll be right there," Val said before spinning back toward Twyla.

He took hold of her hand, guiding her away from the group. "I'm not sure when I'll get away, but I'll call you, okay?"

She searched his eyes. They were filled with darkness, concern, and hesitation with no hint of enthusiasm for the job they'd just accomplished in banishing the demons. In all fairness, he was probably distracted by the job he still had to finish with Payton.

"Sure." She nodded even though the *I'll call you* felt as if he were putting distance between them, blowing her off. Swallowing, she watched his fingers slip from hers. Her jubilation from moments ago slipped away like a deflated balloon.

As soon as Val and Trevor left, ushering Payton back to jail, the Paranormal Council gathered around the firestone.

"Well, at least now we have some confirmation of Payton's culpability," Nora pointed out. "He *had* been stockpiling the cobine—just for the demons."

"I suspect he was supplying to both veaklings and demons," Nate said.

"In my opinion, it's enough to send him to the Condemned Dimension," Sissy added. She stretched her wings, scraping off a clump of demon blood from the feathers and dropping it onto the grass.

The Condemned Dimension. Twyla reflected on the insufferable world. Almost all supernatural beings knew of the place criminal offenders were sent to when banished from the natural earth. She tried to recall the lore describing it as a trapping one couldn't escape from, an island surrounded by nothingness. No one knew for sure, though, because once a being went there, they didn't return.

"What if Payton's goal is to raise an army of miscreants? What if he's using the cobine to control them? What if he wants evil to overthrow good?" Diego asked. "If we send him now, we've lost a connection, a chance of discovering what's afoot."

Omar wiped his blade. "I agree."

"Let's take a vote," Nora instructed. "All those in favor of sending Payton to the Condemned Dimension, show your hand."

Twyla felt like the outsider she was. Stepping out of the circle, she hugged herself, a sense of exhaustion overcoming her. The energy she had expelled fighting the demon was catching up to her. She knew what they were deciding was important, but she just wanted to go home, recuperate, and throw her arms around Val.

Sissy and Annabelle extended their hands into the circle.

"And those who feel we should keep Payton imprisoned here?" Nora asked. The remainder of the group put their hands out, creating the majority of the vote. Nora nodded. "Okay. He stays until we unearth whatever secrets he's keeping... Is he growing a clandestine evil faction—one unknown to us? If so, where are they? Who are they?"

Twyla must have made a noise because her mother turned concerned eyes on her. "And like it or not, it seems Twyla is embroiled in this issue due to her connection with Payton."

Sissy tucked her angel wings against her back. "Perhaps we should make her an honorary member of the Council. That way, she can attend meetings and keep abreast of what we discover."

"That's a good idea," Nora said. Then, to Twyla, she asked, "What do you think?"

Drawing a deep breath, Twyla swept her gaze over the Council members. "That would be fine." She liked everyone here. Plus, she respected the way each one looked after the interests of their own kinds.

Nora put her honorary membership to a vote, which unanimously passed. Twyla nodded, inwardly pleased. It felt good to belong to something bigger than herself.

"We made a good team today," Diego said to the group with his usual enthusiasm. "Reminded me of the old days."

The Council members dispersed, a few walking together into the darkness beyond the light of the firestone.

"Are you all right?" Nora asked.

Twyla expelled a heavy sigh as if a boulder sat on her chest. "I didn't realize the extent of the responsibility I'd be under when I put a spell on that Ruin Coin. For a year, I've been tied to that vampire. I'm ready to be free of him."

"Ah, every spell binds you to a purpose. Did you miss that lesson in the book of spells?" Nora smiled knowingly. "Some can last a lifetime. It's one of the reasons we must wield our power with care."

Twyla's stomach churned, a queasy sensation making her uncomfortable. She nodded, trying to pull herself together. She was confused, wondering what this turn of events meant for her and Val—if it even meant anything. For a moment, her heart squeezed as she thought of Val and how they both had responsibilities. He'd chosen his job over her before. She'd been hurt and resentful. Now she thought she understood. She had a sense she owed allegiance to a cause bigger than herself. For the good of the community.

Would their relationship be able to withstand both their causes? Twyla thought it might. She was happy she could do her part to share in his fight for good.

Val locked Payton in his cell. The vampire had been closemouthed about how he had escaped, smirking at Val's questions. "Wouldn't you like to know?" he'd said.

Well, yes, Val would. Somehow, the demons had gotten Payton out and slipped by Trevor. Val didn't think it could happen again, but he'd still like the intel.

When he went back up to his office, he called Nora. "Could you come by to destroy the pentagram portal?" he asked.

"Can it wait until tomorrow?"

He knew it would be an inconvenience for her to come now, but he didn't want to wait. They'd dispatched the demons back to their world, but what if they simply returned...perhaps angrier than ever? This was out of his area of expertise. "No," he said.

During the long pause on the phone, Val could hear his heart thumping. He'd been going nonstop for hours, and he was tired. Nora most likely shared his exhaustion.

Finally, she relented with a sigh. "Okay. I guess you're right. I'll be there as soon as I can."

After he hung up, he told Trevor, "Nora will be here shortly. Wait here in the office, please. You can catch a catnap while you wait. Until that pentagram is gone, I'm going to hang out in the cell."

"Okay," Trevor said, then slowly headed for the door. He turned, his expression quizzical. "What's to keep him from creating another one?"

"Good question. I'll confer with Nora. She knows more about that kind of stuff than I do."

Trevor nodded before leaving.

Val traipsed back through the tunnels, then entered the vacant *premium* cell down the hall from where Payton was locked up. Val stood over the pentagram, wondering if another demon could appear. He didn't see why not. Removing a white pillowcase from the bed, he sprinkled it with the holy water he still had in his pocket, then covered the star on the floor with it. He was only guessing the move would deter any demon action. Next, he turned the bedside table upside down on top of the pillowcase. The extra cover might keep the holy water moist longer while creating another layer of protection. If something came through, at least he wouldn't miss it.

A few feet away, he fell onto the mattress, stretched out, and placed his hands behind his head. From where he rested, his gaze fell on the table legs, standing like miniature pillars in the air. Now to stay awake.

Twyla's face appeared in his mind. What was she doing? He wished he were with her instead of in this cell. How he would love to cuddle with her to make sure she was okay after all that had happened tonight.

She had been magnificent while wielding her magic. A sense of pride washed over him. She had acted with bravery and passion—his beautiful witch.

He longed to go to her to tell her that he loved her.

Payton made a rude noise that echoed down the hallway. "Hey, you still there?"

But his duty was here. Val gave a weary sigh.

"Spectacular. I get a babysitter now," Payton called from his cell, interrupting Val's quiet reflection.

Val didn't acknowledge him. If he did, Payton's tormenting would never end. As it was, the vampire droned on for an hour or more. Val tuned him out as best he could. His eyes dipped closed, but he fought sleep. He imagined flying in his dragon form, whisking Twyla away on his back.

Hurry, Nora, please hurry.

Nora showed up at the sheriff's office a couple of hours later. It was after two in the morning when Trevor called him on the hand radio to let him know they were heading down. Trevor escorted her into the jail quarters, and Val met them at the entrance. The hour wouldn't seem unusual, considering many supernatural beings tended to be creatures of the night. However, that wasn't the case with witches and dragons. They enjoyed the daylight.

He wondered what had taken her so long.

"I'm sorry for bringing you out so late. Thanks for coming," Val said. She wore her hair pulled up rite so the black tips were tucked in, and all that framed her face was gray. The style was becoming, a much more controlled look than when her hair was down.

"You're welcome. Although I didn't see I had much choice given our demon problem," Nora said from the doorway.

As she stepped into the outer room, Twyla came in and stood beside her mother. He hadn't noticed how similar their features were until this moment. She also had her hair styled on top of her head with a flowered clip dotted with rough-hewn gemstones. But it was the set of her chin and the determined look in her eyes that showed the remarkable resemblance between mother and daughter.

"I didn't expect to see you," he said to Twyla.

She opened her arms with her palms up. "Well, here I am."

"I'm glad to see you've recovered from the battle so quickly," he said.

Nora gave a slight chuckle. "Where's the pentagram?"

Val's mouth quirked to the side. *Straight to business.*

He led her toward the appropriate cell. As soon as they were in the vicinity, Payton laughed. "More visitors. How kind of you."

"I'm not in the mood to deal with you," she said to Payton as he peered through the bars a few yards away. With a wave of her hand, a stone wall erected between Payton and where they stood.

"Nice," Val said. "This way." He directed her into the cell Payton had occupied for nearly a year.

When they reached the pentagram, she pursed her lips. Together, they stared at the star in silence. "What do you think?" he finally inquired.

"Twyla had asked my opinion the other day. I told her it didn't matter, to leave the star alone. I was wrong to say to let it remain."

"Can you get rid of it?"

"Yes. I brought Twyla along to learn the process. We haven't had to deal with this for so long that she hasn't had any experience in thwarting demons."

"I don't know if you'd trust me wielding that much power," Twyla said.

"You're getting better. Look how well you did last night." Nora gave a reassuring pat on her daughter's shoulder.

All this talk about power made Val uneasy. They were in a confined space. How was this going to work?

"Step back, please," Nora said. They did. Val was close enough to reach out and touch Twyla. He wanted to. His fingers itched to rub her back and draw her nearer, but he resisted.

Nora removed a twisted wand from her pocket, then held the tip up in the air as she chanted words in a language he didn't understand. She scraped the tip over the star, healing the stone floor as the symbol ignited before vaporizing, erasing the pentagram and circle. "There," she said, turning.

"Thanks," Val said again. "I owe you one."

She stepped back, glancing from Twyla to him. "And I may collect, soon." She paused as if reconsidering. "Oh, never mind."

He wondered what she'd been about to say. Had it been something to do with Twyla? Was everything okay after last night? He didn't mention her daughter, though. This was work. Best keep it that way. "Can Payton make fashion another star to summon a demon?"

"Of course. If someone is determined to connect with the Dark Realm, they will. That's part of the reason we exile chronic offenders to the Condemned Dimension. They can't affect us from there. There is no access to our dimension…no way to return here, no way to influence anyone here. It's a life sentence."

"Then let's send him on his way," Val said.

Twyla crossed her arms over her chest. "That won't happen for a while. Since it appears Payton has been giving cobine to demons, the Council voted to hold him longer. We believe there's a buildup of evil, and that Payton has a hand in it. We need to learn more for the sake of everyone in Terror."

From the corner of the room, Trevor groaned. Val had almost forgotten he was still there.

"And he needs to remain in prison?" Val asked, his voice rising in frustration. Did they realize how difficult it was to hold a vampire? "The Council should be more aggressive in their pursuit of answers. They need to sentence him or let him go." It was his job to confine the suspect. It was their job to decide what happened to him.

"No," Payton screamed. "Let me go free." His voice and rage filled the entire cave, shaking the internal walls of the cell units. There was no sign of the wisecracks he'd flung earlier. Indeed, Val feared it was the sound and fury of a vampire who'd been pushed to the brink.

"We will speed up the process, I promise," Nora said, looking concerned.

Again, Payton roared like a mad beast. The crash of falling brick and mortar hitting the ground ripped through the room, crunching and cracking as it tumbled to the ground.

Cave-in, Val thought.

Trevor's eyes popped open wide. Twyla covered her mouth with her hand. Nora's gaze bore into him. "What the hell?" Val said. He rushed out the door. The others followed right behind him.

Twyla came to an abrupt halt behind Val. The wall Nora had built in front of the cell had crumbled into a pile of rubble. How had that happened? Had Payton's bellow processed that much energy and been powerful enough to do it? It was the only explanation she could think of to cause this sort of destruction.

Stunned, she swept her gaze over the area. The jail structure had been compromised where the bricks had fallen. The ends of the metal bars were pulled loose of the rocks that held them. Twyla followed the yawning gap, glancing into the empty cell. "Where is Payton?"

"I don't know. Stay back," Val instructed, throwing an outstretched arm between them.

A skirmish came from behind them. Twyla spun around at the same time as Val. The situation was bad. Trevor, nearest to her, had fallen back against the stone wall of the cave. Payton had somehow maneuvered behind them. He had Nora imprisoned with his arm clutched around her neck, tugging her backward so she was off balance. With his other hand, he struck her arm with such force it caused her to release her wand.

"Let her go," Twyla yelled.

Val took a step forward.

"Stay where you are, dragon," Payton said. "Move and I'll snap her neck."

Twyla felt the blood drain from her face. The Ruin Coin around his neck kept him from tracing, but it did little to subdue his mighty strength.

Val froze.

"Witch, if you want your mother to live, then you'll remove the Ruin Coin and its spell," Payton ordered. "Now."

"All right." She swallowed her fear for her mother. On the inside, Twyla's wrath built and bubbled like a volcano. How dare the vampire lay a hand on Nora! Twyla closed her hands into fists. Her focus was solely on Payton's eyes, watching him. She lifted her burning palms, taking a slow step forward. "Let me…"

"Twyla don't," Val said, taking another step.

"I have to," she replied.

"Dragon, stop." Payton peered at Trevor. "And you, go stand over there by your sheriff."

Trevor did as he was told.

"Now slowly, Twyla. Come to me."

She took careful steps, not exactly sure what she was going to do when she reached him. He was strong. She could see the veins in her mother's neck straining as she resisted his pull. Nora whimpered. The sound caused Twyla to snap. In the blink of an eye, she whirled on Payton, swinging her fist up and around to release a burst of fire and energy on his head. It shot down through his body to the ground like a bolt of lightning in its intensity.

Payton collapsed. Nora stumbled free, catching herself against the wall. Val bounded forward in an instant, wielding his velum. He thrust it deep into Payton's heart, going to his knees with the force of the blow.

Payton's eyes flung open wide before closing for good. His body disintegrated into ash and fell to the stone floor.

Twyla scanned her mother for injuries. She was breathing hard, they all were, but Nora was okay. "I had to kill him. It was the only way."

Val stood. "You didn't kill him. I did."

She blinked. Was he trying to take the blame? How would the Council react? "He was dead before he hit the ground, and you know it."

"I had to make sure." He closed the distance between them. Resting his hands on her shoulders, he gazed into her eyes. "You were in danger. And I protect what's mine."

She smiled tentatively. *Was* she his?

He kissed her forehead, her cheek, and then his mouth closed over hers in a possessive kiss.

"Uh…. I've been in the cave long enough," Nora said.

Val wrapped an arm around Twyla's waist, holding her as her pulse settled.

"What do we do with the ashes?" Trevor asked.

"I'll speak with Nathaniel in the morning. We'll let him deal with the remains. As a vampire, he can handle arrangements."

"How do you think the veakling community will react?" Twyla asked. "Will they retaliate?"

"Let me handle them," Nora said.

"And the Council, too," Twyla added.

"Yes, the Council also."

Trevor glanced around at the rubble. "I'm not looking forward to cleaning this up."

"Sorry, I'm all out of magic for today," Nora said, pushing strands of hair off her face.

Trevor led the group through the tunnel to the sheriff's office.

"You can stay. See if you can catch some sleep. I'll escort Nora and Twyla home, then return later in the morning.

"Gotcha."

Val slid his palm into Twyla's, folding his fingers around hers. He brought her hand up, pressing his lips to the back of it. "Remind me not to get on your bad side."

14

Twyla ran the soil through her fingers. She felt the need to dance with the earth today. Tossing handfuls of dirt haphazardly into clay pots, she turned and swirled to the rhythm she heard in her head. She'd exceeded her expectations in the fight against the demons the night before. She'd been shocked by her power and how alive it had made her feel. But, at the same time, she felt a pang of remorse over taking a life. She hadn't anticipated the guilt.

Today, though, the delightful sensations of manipulating the forces remained with her. Never in her life had she experienced such a deep calling. She wondered if this was how magic made her mother feel. Twyla longed to share her discovery with Val, but he hadn't come to see her. His absence filled her with doubt. When would the memory of their past breakup leave her in peace?

Uncertain, she turned to what she knew best—the earth and her garden. Taking a deep breath, she turned her face up to the sun's warmth. It was time to plant the watermelon seedlings she'd started in the greenhouse a month or so ago.

After she loaded the wheelbarrow, she set off to the raised garden plot at the far end of the garden. She knelt and dug small holes, then set the seedlings inside and watered them. Her usual sense of pleasure nudged upward like an opening sunflower. Determined not to allow anyone to take control of her happiness, she finished planting the entire watermelon plot, not looking at her phone a single time.

As she stood to admire her progress, she noticed someone approaching. An instant memory of Ethan kidnapping her surfaced. A wave of fear slammed into her, but she shoved it away. She squinted at the figure. She recognized that swagger, even from this distance. It was Val.

*

Golden rays of sunlight spilled over Twyla's hair, reflecting its ink-black silkiness. As he approached, Val wanted to unravel the ties and let the strands fall about her shoulders. She was gorgeous in her jeans and a tan T-shirt that read, *100% Natural Beauty.*

He had been busy over the last day working with Nathaniel and making sure Payton's ashes were returned to the veakling vampires. That entire ordeal had made him overthink how he'd handled things. Should he have even taken the vampire out of his cell to begin with? Had he gotten too involved with Twyla? Had it clouded his judgment? Finally, he decided it didn't matter. He had chased her away before because of some misplaced notion that his job defined him. He realized now how vital Twyla was to him. And he could handle duty and love—it wasn't an either-or situation.

He swung a picnic basket as he walked.

She tossed her head back, shading her eyes. "I thought you might be hungry," he said.

"I am. I didn't eat breakfast." Her voice sounded sweet and happy.

He took her hand, then led her into the shade of a nearby tree. Dragging her up against him with one arm, he kissed her long and hard.

A raspy breath escaped her lips when he released her. "I thought you were pushing me away again," she whispered.

"I'm sorry. That was never my intent," he said, holding her gaze. "I love you, Twyla. I've been fighting it for a long time, but I can't anymore. I love you more than anything—including my job."

She grinned, her eyes glowing. "I never asked you to give up your job."

He nodded, feeling almost embarrassed. "I know. It was me...all me. Somehow, I got it in my head that I had to choose. But I'm over it now."

She leaned in, kissing him while threading her hands in his hair. When the kiss ended, she asked, "Are you going to put that basket down?"

"I am. I packed it myself with all your favorite things. I even picked up graveyard greens from Beauty & Beast." He opened the basket, retrieved a blanket, and spread it over the ground.

She inhaled melodramatically, teasing him. "That proves it—you must love me. And I-I love you, my dragon."

He smiled, his heart full. Pulling her to him, he kissed her soundly, then eased her down onto the blanket. He wasn't hungry for food anymore. Only for Twyla.

Trevor's feet were propped on the desk when Val escorted Twyla into the sheriff's office. He sat up straight, his shoes hitting the floor with a *kerplop*. It had been three weeks since the incident with the demons, and though they had been waiting for something more to happen, nothing had.

"Hi, Twyla. Val," Trevor said as he smoothed his hair back.

Twyla waved at him.

"How's it going?" Val asked.

Trevor shrugged. "About the usual."

"Good." Val took his badge off, then handed it to Trevor. "I'm going out of town for a week or so. That makes you acting sheriff."

Trevor's jaw dropped, shocked, before he snapped it closed. "Do you think that's wise? You know…"

"Terror is forever at risk. It's the nature of the town," Val said. "But you can handle it."

Nodding, Trevor stood. "All right, then. Don't you worry about a thing." His gaze shot from Twyla to Val with a sly grin. "Just have yourselves a good time. You deserve it."

"Thanks. I have some catching up to do." Val kissed Twyla's brow.

The pair headed for the door, but Trevor stopped them. "Hey, where are you going?" he asked.

Val smiled, nudging Twyla's hip playfully. "It's a secret."

"Aw, come on. Tell me," Trevor said.

Twyla shot him a wink. "Nocturne Falls. They say it's a fabulous place."

THE END

Thank you for reading *Forever at Risk*. If you enjoyed this story and want to stay up-to-date on my next book and release dates then sign up for my newsletter. (I promise your email address will never be shared and you can unsubscribe at any time.)

https://larissaemerald.com/contact/

Did you know that one of most awesome things you can do for an author is post a review? It doesn't need to be long, just a few lines will do, but a review goes a long way to help authors achieve visibility. So, if you enjoyed the book, share the news with a friend and take a few minutes to leave a review!

Read on for a sneak peek of **Perfection**.

Excerpt from

PERFECTION

CODE PERFECT SERIES

LARISSA EMERALD

CHAPTER 1

May 1, 2226

In a proficient dance of gears and balance, the robotic waitress slid breakfast onto the table before rolling away from the booth. Eggs, spinach, buffalo sausage, and coffee—his usual. Lieutenant York Richmond wrapped his fingers around the steaming cup of cloned Colombian, forgoing the undersized handle, and drew it to his lips. The steam, along with the familiar aroma, awakened his sinuses. Now if only it would nudge his brain and muscles to life.

"Rough night, huh?" Across from him, Detective Vivian Lester lined up her silverware on the table, then picked up the spoon and stirred cream into her coffee.

He shrugged at his partner's understatement. "Need to change families for a month or so, s'all."

"Guess it's kind of weird to arrest your mom."

"Well, you know Mom. Queen of protests." His mother fought for equality between Genetically Engineered Individuals and Coders, the descendants of the original human gene pool. She hated the direction of designer babies and the Committee's regulations that governed GEI and everyone else.

"Hey, there's an antiquities sale tomorrow. Want to go?"

He set aside the coffee, hit his eggs with equal shots of

Tabasco and mustard, and dug in. If Vi felt compelled to divert his attention to his hobby, then he must be a seriously sorry sight. His mouth edged into a reluctant smile, despite how tired he felt. "I'm good."

"Really?"

"Besides, I didn't arrest her. Technically, anyway. I just ensured she wasn't newsworthy by calming her down." The national media weren't after the truth—they were after a story. He stabbed his fork into a hunk of sausage, slid the utensil between his teeth, left the meat behind, and removed the metal. Peering at her across the table, he quirked a single brow.

With a contrite nod, she turned her attention to her French toast.

Vi treating him like a keepsake Christmas ornament was over. Really, she wanted to go hunting for antiques with him? Ever since Danny—

No. He put the brakes on that thought. Tapping his spot computer, he rested it in his palm as he searched the Chicago headlines for any sign of Amanda Richmond. *Nothing.*

Good for you, Mom.

The headlines focused on the World Health Organizations US regional convention, which was where his mother had been protesting. The broadcast showed dignitaries exchanging greetings. GEI and Coders filled the expansive hall at the Rhodium Hotel. To the casual eye, they seemed similar with their homogenized honey-brown skin from the mixed races blending over the years. But that was where the resemblances ended. Unlike throughout history, today's issue wasn't about race—it was about privilege. His mom was outspoken about equal genetic opportunities and restricting the push for more advancement.

He checked a few more sites for any different news, then paused. On the screen, a newscaster announced the discovery of yet another suicide by genetic mutation.

Instances of people shooting up with a genetic-alteration serum had reached epidemic proportions. The serum caused their genes to go haywire and mutate until they died, horribly. A shiver raced through him. He was glad he hadn't caught that case. It hit too close to home.

"So you want to go chumming around with me tomorrow, eh?" he asked.

Vi rolled her eyes.

He half chuckled. "I thought so. We could even make it a family affair—hook up with Mom, cousin Stacey, and the kids. Maybe even Cal."

"Let's leave your brother out of it. It's not Christmas or anyone's birthday, so I'm good." She stared at her breakfast as if engrossed. That was the problem with friends dating family. When the relationship didn't work out, things got awkward. Cal wanted Vi to quit the force. Vi didn't want to. End of relationship.

An announcement from the International Security Intelligence Generator of Human Tracking overrode York's info search, shocking the amused grin right off his face. The forkful of Tabasco-laced eggs he'd been eager to consume a millisecond earlier didn't make it into his mouth. He lowered his arm, the fork clanking against plastic. The sausage in his mouth turned bland and grainy, much like eating sand. The food scraped his throat as he swallowed. "What the hell?"

"What? Not your mom?"

"No. A message from InSIGHT." In disbelief, he read the accompanying post aloud, his appetite shriveling with every syllable. "Isabelle D-Gastion is dead."

Vi gasped. "That's impossible. She's GEI."

"Right, and genetically engineered individuals don't die without help, what with their perfect genes and all." York thumbed the valet button synced to his air-car's autopilot. "I've signaled for the car. Ready?" He scooted to the end of the booth, then stood.

"Guess so. Where are we going?"

"Fredrick B-Gastion's." His tone grim, he said, "If I've learned anything in the last few years, it's there's a first time for everything. And given she's the daughter of the World Health Organization's regional director, well, this can't be an accident."

Poor, innocent Isabelle. She was only two. He drew a deep breath. It felt like a heavy hand pressed over his heart.

As they exited the diner, a vocal emergency statement came through his comm, instructing them to report to the scene. Good thing, considering he was heading there anyway. Fredrick was a friend.

Daylight had broken, but, from where they stood, skyscrapers hid the sun. This early in the morning, the city still slept. In an hour or so, the streets and walkways would be bustling with people. For an instant, he was aware of the changing of the guard, so to speak. The hum of huge air purification filters on the nearby corner ceased. Chicago sat silent, expectant. He breathed in a whiff of smog-free air. This quiet moment rang false. Every part of him knew it.

His air-car pulled up to the curb, and they got in. After adjusting the thrusters for vertical ascent, he launched. Memos flashed over a nucleus screen set in the console, and his onboard computer kept up a running monologue of information and updates as he drove. The female voice sounded cool and collected. By the time he'd piloted from midtown to the swanky Chicago suburb on the lake, three notices indicated other units had arrived at the Gastion residence

He gripped the steering wheel. Had the child died of natural causes—which seemed impossible unless there'd been some sort of accident—or was someone targeting her father and the kid had gotten in the way? The WHO's regional director held jurisdiction over the Committee and its genetic selections, oversaw universal health emergencies, monitored the impact of climate and environmental change, and advocated for the Coder population. Dealing with those issues placed Fredrick B-Gastion in direct conflict with a lot of people. Was someone upset about a decision WHO had made? Were they angry enough to retaliate?

"Hand it over, ladybug," Kindra B-Zaika said with a gentle tone meant to coax her child into minding.

"No." Brianna stomped her foot, defiantly throwing her head back.

Stunned by her daughter's uncharacteristic explosive outburst, Kindra inhaled a calming breath.

"I want it to open *noooow*," Brianna wailed, drawing the final word into a quivering, nerve-scraping bleat.

Kindra touched cool fingers to her brow, then glanced out the panel of windows in the living room to discover dawn tiptoeing over the city. A streak of air traffic blazed in the distance, weaving between skyscrapers. People were on the move. But here she was, stonewalled by a two-year-old. She couldn't leave for work with Brianna so upset.

Her daughter held out the potted sunflower in her small hands. Her eyes glistened as her blue irises disappeared into rich-brown outer rims—a telltale sign of how distraught she was.

"The flower has a growth cycle. It's not time for it to bloom," Kindra explained.

Brianna thrust out her lower lip, then pitched the uncooperative plant to the floor. Kindra sighed, struggling for composure as she watched the melodrama of flailing arms and legs that followed. She'd never encountered such a tantrum, so she wasn't sure how to deal with it. What was happening to her sweet little girl? Such out-of-control behavior was a first. In fact, they'd bred D-Generation to have an even temperament.

Worried, Kindra folded her hands, then touched a

knuckle to her lips. She was reluctant to play the waiting game, but what else could she do? She tried to think of solutions, from sending Brianna to timeout to making her clean up the mess to scolding her. But she was only two. Would those punishments even work?

It'll pass.

Kindra had a gazillion items on her overloaded agenda. Just the thought of presenting her controversial report to the Genetics Committee right when she arrived at the office made her shudder. Nausea roiled in her stomach. The Committee had gotten power hungry lately, and they didn't care to have their authority challenged. She needed quiet. She needed solitude. She needed to rehearse her pitch.

"Fifteen minutes," Nanny Sally advised as she entered the room.

"Yes, I know," Kindra said when the popular-model android began to tick off five-minute increments in an effort to get her to work on time. *Fooltar.* She could do without the nanny's annoying programming this morning.

Near the electric-blue sofa, she knelt beside her daughter. A thrashing foot clipped Kindra's shin, snagging her leggings. She winced, then stroked Brianna's forehead. *Be calm, please.*

Brianna stilled at her mother's touch, turning big, watery eyes up.

"Ladybug, you can't *make* the flower bloom just because you want it to."

With several hiccups, Brianna tried to control her crying.

Kindra collected the pot, replaced a handful of spilled soil, and set it upright on the floor. She settled cross-legged next to the plant, then spied the gel book on the end table. Perhaps a pretend flower would do in the interim. She extended her hand, concentrated, and summoned Brianna's holographic computer with a flare of psychokinesis.

Stilling, Brianna peered at her. She sniffed back tears with sudden interest.

Kindra smothered a thankful sigh. Distraction. Perfect. She skipped her fingers over the gel book, bringing the electronic images to life until she accessed the file she wanted. "What color would you like your flower to be?"

"Yellow. Intense yellow."

Intense, of course—Brianna's word of the week. Last week, it was *activate*. A rush of pride swelled inside Kindra at her daughter's advanced intelligence. All children of D-Generation were geniuses, as mandated by the Committee. They would be attend university by age nine.

Kindra sighed. *Such potential.*

These kids were far beyond what she had been as a child, more intelligent, more intuitive, and more talented. Even though Kindra graduated high school at thirteen, university at seventeen, and worked alongside her father learning the ins and outs of genetics, she wondered if she had even a hope of keeping up when the Ds grew into adults.

With another swirl of her finger, a vibrant sunflower popped up from the page. Kindra carefully detached the 3D creation, separating it from the book. "This will have to do until I get home this evening."

"But it's May Day. I wanted to give you a *real* flower."

Downy, soul-deep warmth caressed Kindra's insides. "I appreciate that. But some things can't be rushed." She smiled. The urge to stay home from work tempted her. "Come here." She patted her leg, inviting Brianna to sit on her lap.

Her little girl scooted over, sniffled again, then snuggled closer, surveying the wounded plant. Kindra caressed her sweet oval face, smoothing silky strands of blond hair away from eyes that were gradually returning to their lively crystal blue. Like mother, like daughter. Brianna was sensitive, intuitive, and demanding. Kindra smiled, amazed at how a genetically engineered D-Generation— one far superior to her own B-Generation—were created with such scientific precision, yet remained so defined by age emotionally.

"I'll bring a freshly blooming flower home with me when I return from work, okay? This one"—she firmly tamped down the soil around the base of the stem—"will take a few days to open."

Brightening, Brianna tilted her head with an impish nod. "Not a cloned one."

Where do kids learn these things?

"I'll do my best." Kindra wrapped her arms around Brianna, breathing in her little-girl scent. When had this child she'd rescued from the embryo-discard bin come to mean so much to her? It had been an impulsive, weak moment. The Committee had discarded so many embryos. Kindra had felt if she could save at least one, it would fill the void inside her. But as time passed and she learned more about being a mother, the more her discontent with the Committee grew.

Brianna filled Kindra's heart with love, leaving it aching in its intensity. Had her own mother ever cared for her this way?

Doesn't matter.

She shook her head when Brianna wiggled out of her arms. Clearly ready to play, her child swept up a doll from a nearby chair.

Kindra stood. "How about if you and Chloe do a unity session? The quiet time will help you center yourself."

Brianna headed down the hall without a backward glance. "Can't," she said before disappearing through her bedroom door, Chloe hugged to her chest.

Kindra's breath snagged in her throat, and she frowned. Brianna had never refused the spiritual exercise. Another warning signal tripped—an additional odd occurrence. First the tantrum. Now this.

With her usual rigid posture and head tilt that didn't displace a single dark hair, Sally held out a square box housing Kindra's computer key, the coded chip she needed to access files at work. "Time to go."

Fingers curling around it, Kindra ripped her attention from her daughter. "Call me if she gets upset again."

"I will. Don't forget my updated replacement arrives tomorrow."

"Yes. I have it in my system," Kindra said absently, grabbing her satchel from the foyer table. As she closed the door behind her, she couldn't shake the mother's intuition telling her something bigger was wrong with Brianna.

She shook her head. Perhaps it was simply growing pains. Brianna had a birthday soon.

He jogged up to Gina just as she was unlocking the apartment door. She jumped. He took hold of her hands, pulling her abruptly toward him. As he was a little winded and a lot exited, a moment passed before he could speak. "It's done."

"What are you talking about?" Blankly, she stared, leaning backward so her sunflower-blonde hair draped down her back. Her fine, sculptured brows knit with confusion.

He wanted to grab a fistful of hair and tug her into submission, but he resisted. He was a man of willpower, after all. Didn't his planning and careful execution of his idea prove that?

"Remember when I mentioned I'd discovered a way to make them pay for their slights over the years? To once and for all show them I was just as smart and capable as their top scientists?" *God, he longed to share his accomplishment. She'd be so proud of him.*

"What did you do?" she asked hesitantly.

Smoothing his fingers over her cheek, he changed his mind about telling her. He didn't want anything to dampen his mood, his elation. "Nothing. Never mind. We'll talk about it tomorrow." He interlocked his fingers with hers, then led her into the apartment and his bedroom.

CHAPTER 2

York parked alongside B-Gastion's Air-Porsche on the second floor of the landing garage, as he had for past visits. He admired the Porsche while he and Vi strolled between the vehicles. B-Gastion had chosen a fancy family flyer while York had gone for sleek power.

"You're going to get in trouble for parking here," Vi complained.

"Maybe. But I don't think the captain's speech about not ruffling the locals' feathers referred to active investigations."

They didn't speak as they navigated the stairs to a private access. A wall of shrubbery kept them hidden until they were almost to the front door. A crowd had gathered halfway up the walkway, which was framed by low, manicured hedges. Vehicles filled the street. "Damn. Every reporter in town must have intercepted the police stream."

"Better here than at your mom's arrest. Benefited her situation, don't you think?"

"Nah, too much time had lapsed. Just a lucky break." But this morning *had* been too easy. Coincidence? The media types trolled for headlines, and they had the money to support their efforts. Of course, GEIs were far too interested in what was happening in their own circles to invest much effort in the imperfect world of Coders. But…

Screw it. York had other worries right now.

His spot computer thrummed against his hand. He checked it while he walked. The data readout darkened, adjusting to the sunlight piercing the clouds in the east. InSIGHT had updated the status of Isabelle's investigation with photos and preliminary stats of body temperature and decomposition. York studied the images of tiny Isabelle lying on the floor of a child's bedroom, a doll clutched to her chest. A knot lodged in his throat. He shivered, and his stomach clenched. York wouldn't wish this tragedy on the genetic misfits hiding in the tunnels, let alone on a valued friend.

As regional director, B-Gastion had built strong partnerships with other nations committed to accelerating progress toward global development goals of health surveillance and reducing health inequalities. In the eighty years or so since the GEIs had stepped into the vast majority of power jobs in society, the position had been held by a GEI, and his policy usually favored the wealthy. Even so, when York's boy was ill, B-Gastion was the only GEI who attempted to help him.

York inhaled a breath, held it, then moved on with the exhale. He could feel Vi watching him, probably wondering how he was holding up. *Solid,* he wanted to tell her, but he didn't.

Beneath the stately columned portico, Fredrick B-Gastion greeted them with the formality one would expect from a dignitary. His spine held him erect, but the forward dip of his shoulders and grief in his eyes gave him away. "Thank you for coming so promptly, Lieutenant."

"Of course." York clasped his friend's extended hand. "I'm not sure if you've met my partner, Detective Vivian Lester."

"I have, but I can't remember where at the moment."

Vi angled her head. "I wish this meeting were under different circumstances, sir."

Didn't they all?

No matter appearances, B-Gastion had to feel hurt and broken. The evidence rang clear in the regional director's half-hearted handshake and emotion-reddened eyes.

"Let's go inside." York urged B-Gastion toward the half-open door.

Vi trailed them. Their feet rapped an uneven rhythm on the glossy marble tiles as they moved deeper into the house. He and B-Gastion stopped when they reached the living area. They stared at each other, professional to professional, man to man, father to father.

"Who made the discovery?" York asked. The anguish on B-Gastion's face said he may have reached his threshold for holding it together. York placed an arm around his friend's shoulder, then directed him toward the sofa. B-Gastion pulled away without taking a seat.

"Her mother." B-Gastion's voice broke on the last word, and he cleared his throat. "How...how could this happen? It's not supposed to happen."

York smothered a curse. "We'll find out. I'm so sorry."

"This is... It's such a shock." Fredrick pressed his lips together, then averted his eyes.

"The sooner we start the investigation, the quicker we'll have answers," Vi said gently. "Where's Isabelle's room?"

Fredrick glanced at the staircase. His face crumpled, mouth quivering.

York stood tall, wishing he could loan his friend his strength. "We can find our way. Why don't you sit for a few?"

Drawing a breath, B-Gastion appeared to suck back his emotion as best he could. "No. No, I should go with you."

"It's all right. The ME and the forensic team will arrive soon. You can usher them in." York sought words of comfort, but he knew it was impossible. Condolences wouldn't grant B-Gastion what he wanted most. So York slipped a recorder ring from his finger and held it out, a stall technique to give the other man time to compose himself. "Dictate every detail you can remember. The daily routine. If anyone new has been in the house. Anything and everything."

B-Gastion took the ring, then eased it over his thumb with shaky fingers.

A few minutes later, York and Vi stood in the center of the dead two-year-old's room. Inconceivable. Sprawled on the floor, she looked so alone dressed in her pale pink pajamas covered in cartoons renditions of black-and-white kittens. Tightening his hold on his crime-scene kit, he struggled for perspective. If he could shut out the sound of weeping coming from the room next door—surely B-Gastion's wife—it would make his task a hell of a lot easier.

He knelt beside the Isabelle's D-Gastions small body. Blond hair framed a delicate face, brushing her shoulders. The child could have been in a deep sleep, hugging a lookalike Global Doll.

Exhaling a shuddering breath, he fought the sting in his eyes. It had been six years since he'd faced the death of someone this young, and his son's passing had not been so peaceful. His hand shook as he opened the crime-scene bag. Images of his boy flashed in his mind—a toothless grin, a small hand tossing a red ball, thin arms wrapped tightly around his neck.

Briefly, he squeezed his eyes shut before opening them.

The quiet sound of Vi's voice brought his head up. Standing on the opposite side of Isabelle, she dictated information into her spot computer.

She met his gaze. "Hey, I didn't consider it earlier, but why did the captain assign this one to us? It's not our RO."

"Rotation doesn't come into play here. B-Gastion requested me."

She angled her head. "Oh, right."

York sensed her watching him, perhaps searching for a

reaction. He just passed his med-scanner over the girl, watching the monitor for any sign of physical trauma but finding none.

"This doesn't make sense, Vi. No trauma. And GEIs don't die, even in accident situations. Primps can put them back together with cloning and such."

"Unless the injury is to the head. The brain is the one organ that can't be cloned."

The health packages for GEIs far exceeded the basic medical unit of immunity to disease and illness granted to Coders like York. The genetic code of Coders remained largely unaltered. When they did get alterations, they were the kind that attached to stem cells and altered the genes from the outside in, as opposed to the ground-up method from inception used with GEIs. In the early years of genetic engineering, participating in the new science had required money. *Perfection* had cost a hefty sum.

So did saving a life, he thought bitterly. *Even a young one.*

Vi averted her gaze from the girl's body. "Yeah, strange."

After he shoved the test equipment into his bag, he roughly zipped it. "There isn't a mark on her. Nothing."

"Then what killed her?" Vi's voice snagged.

York stood. "You okay?"

She nodded, but avoided eye contact. He knew better than to believe her. It was a code of denial they shared.

"Any guesses?"

Crossing his arms to control the tightness in his chest, he shrugged. "Some sort of asphyxiation, maybe? Poison? I don't know."

His QuL beeped in his ear, and he responded with a brusque, "York."

"When are you going to get rid of that QuickLink? It's a dinosaur," Vi whispered. Then she held up a hand, talking more to herself than to him. "I know, I know. Less likely to be traced by criminals."

He rolled his eyes, focusing on Captain Avery's voice.

As usual, the captain sounded worried. He was probably getting hit from all sides. Damn politics. Avery asked for a crisis update. York obliged with a list of stats. "We're treating this like a suspicious death until we learn differently. We'll check out any contacts. Wait to see if there are demands. Maybe it's extorsion gone bad."

York listened to his superior's instructions. Grimacing, he said, "Right. One of us will go over there."

He disconnected.

"Now what?" Vi asked.

"Avery wants one of us to fetch a geneticist since we don't have an expert on staff. Then take 'em to the morgue to evaluate the...*situation*."

She pursed her lips, then shifted her attention to wrapping up her notes.

"Vi? Talk to me." At her obvious reluctance, he added their customary, "Flip you for it." He withdrew his lucky coin from his pocket. It was a 1976 quarter from the days when they actually used coins.

Slowly, she shook her head.

Finally, she curled her spot computer into her chest. Good thing it was made from flexible materials. It appeared as if she were going to crush it in her hand. Her almond-shaped eyes blazed. "You know how I hate those scientists."

"Like I don't?"

"Will you do it? Please?"

He glanced around the room, taking in the perfect environment of a model GEI child. Just two weeks ago, he'd bounced the sweet, laughing girl on his knee. Something horribly strange was going on. Damn it, for little Isabelle D-Gastion, he would set aside his personal feelings and unearth the truth. He'd work with those high-and-mighty scientists even if it killed him.

"Don't worry. This one's mine." No way he'd be satisfied with anyone else handling the case, anyway. A door clacked shut downstairs, then voices echoed throughout the house—probably the forensic team. "But you owe me a pizza," he added.

"Deal," she said without hesitation. Tucking her hair behind her ear, she forced out a heavy sigh. "Guess we should let go of this hatred eventually."

"Never."

"Did the captain ask for any geneticist in particular?"

York lifted the test bag. "Wouldn't you know—he wants that hardnosed B-Zaika." He didn't know her personally, but the lead scientist of the Seville Genetics Center was always on the news. York could envision her beautiful smile as she hawked her latest creation to the public in her slight English accent.

With an exaggerated consoling pat on the back, Vi said, "Sorry."

"Sure." York thought he heard a good-humored snicker behind him as they stepped out of the bedroom and into the hall. God knew they needed something to ease the sting of leaving that poor little girl behind.

A pair of sweepers arrived first. They would check all the electronics in the room. Next came the ME and a couple of uniforms. York acknowledged Shishido, the officer in charge of the forensics team, then addressed the group. "Test for foreign substances, poison. Check the toys, gel books, clothes, everything. Whatever killed her may be on anything she touched. Take their Nanny Sally back to our lab, too. I want an e-specialist to go over all security and electronics. And we're going to want to talk with anyone who has access to the house."

The others nodded. With a look, he passed the command to Vi, then went downstairs after she took the team into the bedroom. B-Gastion now sat on the sofa where York had left him. There were people moving around him—technicians going over every inch of the place and more uniforms documenting everything, all searching for evidence that would tell them what had killed a GEI child.

Fredrick started to rise, but York motioned for him to stay put. Better to remain out of the techs' way. "You done with that?" he asked, indicating the recorder ring.

Slowly, the dazed man nodded and handed it over.

York slipped it onto his finger. "I'll need to talk to Isabelle's mother, of course, and your staff. Also, I'll need a list of your enemies. People who aren't happy with your policies, whoever you can think of who might want to cause trouble or hurt you, etcetera." His voice softened. "And if you think of anything else, or if there's anything I can do, call me."

B-Gastion rubbed the back of his neck. "Thank you."

York gave a curt nod. "I'll be back later."

Vi waited for him at the gigantic double panel doors. As he walked closer, all the anger and frustration, pain and memories, twisted into a colossal knot in his chest. He'd forgotten rule number one—*don't allow people to get too close because it hurts like hell.*

He thought he'd learned that lesson. He'd thought he was numb.

God, he'd thought *wrong*. His dismay over investigating the death of a child weighed on him. With a white-knuckled grip on the brass handle, he glanced at his partner and threw open the door. "Get ready for the piranhas."

They'd gotten in behind the cover of the landscaping, but exiting would not be so easy.

Vi quickly stepped out, almost breaking into a run. York matched her pace. It was standard in such situations, but that didn't mean he had to like it. They hadn't made it far before reporters bombarded them. Within inches of bursting through the wall of news people lining the pristine lawn, York halted. "Get the hell out of my way."

No one budged. Fine. He'd enjoy mowing them down. It was *that* kind of day.

A cluster of tiny drone cameras—Tracers—hovered overhead. At times like this, York detested procedure. In his experience, rules weren't necessarily the quickest route to satisfactory solutions.

"Move," he bit out more loudly. Dealing with these dipshit reporters wasted time he didn't have. A child was dead, for God's sake. They needed answers ASAP.

Unexpected images from the time surrounding his son's death attacked his mind with strobe-light speed. A final wheeze of breath. Unnatural stillness. The scent of incense at the funeral. York fisted his hands, fingernails digging into his palms.

Danny.

He thrust his hands into his pockets, mentally slamming his son's memory back into its box. That had been another life. Another ambition. Another person. Since Danny's death, York had taken strong measures to avoid cases like this, even going so far as requesting Avery keep him off the death investigations pertaining to children. Yet, here he was, right in the thick of one. Assigned to work with a GEI geneticist to uncover the truth.

A tall reporter, his expression aggressive, tried to block York. "I heard it was the child. Was she in an accident?"

"Take it somewhere else." York gave the man a chance to comply before he tore the Tracer controller, branded with the *Chicago Times* logo, from the guy's hands and flung it. Above, a single drone spiraled out of the pack, plummeted, and crashed into the courtyard's sleek marble fountain.

"Hey!" With a searing glare, the reporter lunged forward. "Lieutenant"—the guy dipped his gaze to read York's ID—"Richmond." He stepped back. "Whose side are you on?"

"The child's." Why did people always reduce genetic issues to *our* side versus *their* side? The shadow of a beard and a slightly darker expression told York that, like himself, the reporter was a Coder. The man was also sturdy and muscular. York forced calm as his instincts prickled. He glanced about.

"Wait… Richmond. Isn't your mother one of the leaders of the anti-GEI movement?" one reporter asked.

The other reporters closed ranks like ants after a legs-up beetle. They spit out question after question.

"Is it true a GEI child died?"

"Isn't that unheard of for Artificial Womb Engineered babies?"

"Can you give us a name? A quote?"

"From which generation? C? D?"

"What does Fredrick B-Gastion have to do with this?"

York felt his spine tighten one vertebra at a time. He lowered a shoulder, then shoved the tall reporter out of the way, ready to linebacker a path to the air-car if necessary.

Central in his mind, though, were the words *why* and *how*.

Why B-Gastion's child and how had this happened?

Vi grabbed a fistful of the back of his shirt. She pulled him to her, saying under her breath, "Easy, York. Captain will be pissed if we're on the twenty-four-hour news."

He twisted around to glare. "Don't give a shit."

"Well, you better."

She was right. He fought his anger, sucking in a deep breath. With his steely gaze fixed on the reporters, he said, "You'll know when we know." To Vi, he muttered, "Happy?"

She gave him a smart-ass smile. Her light brown hair was cut in the latest style—short on one side, then angled down and around to almost brush her shoulder on the other. Her appearance was sharp, like a person who had it together, but she seemed tired. Her green eyes locked on his a second too long, and he glimpsed sadness. Like him, she'd lost a kid after trying some newfangled genetic-enhancement crap. God, if Vi could keep it together while working a case like this, he damn well had to.

He turned his attention to the reporter in the front of the pack. Setting his jaw and fisting his hands, York stared the reporter down until the guy stepped back, creating an opening.

"Let's go." York gestured for Vi to step through the line.

They'd no sooner made it to the air-car before his QuL trilled again. This time, the call was from B-Gastion, asking York if he would personally monitor events at the morgue.

B-Gastion had come to York's aide when he'd been desperate to find help for his son and no one else had given a damn. Now it was time to repay his debt.

He closed his eyes. "Of course. It would be an honor."

When Kindra arrived at Seville, she surged through the door of the spacious laboratory. Late, in a lousy mood, and worried about Brianna's unusual outburst. As she traveled the hallway, the nursery room caught her attention. Peering through the glass windows at the rows and rows of artificial wombs, she sighed, struggling to calm her nerves. At a station at the left, technicians took the genetically modified embryos—the ones she had designed to fit the Committee requirements—and placed them in wombs where they would grow until full term. She thought of all the parents who waited expectantly for their baby. She recalled the foreign yet wonderful feeling she'd had when she'd held Brianna for the first.

Perfection. This was how it should be. She moved on to her office, then dropped her satchel on the curved table that had alternating glass partitions separating the work and comfort stations. Automatically, she took her lab coat off its customary hook and shrugged it on.

An unfamiliar baritone penetrated her thoughts. "I'm looking for Dr. B-Zaika."

Glancing across the room, she froze as she spotted her lab assistant directing a deeply tanned, rock-solid man her way. She had less than a second to scrutinize the stranger: Coder race, dark hair, shadow of beard, and oozing an air of mystery.

He turned toward her, and her knees nearly buckled under the onslaught of his gaze. Exotic and unfamiliar energy fired through her. Being GEI, she was used to perfection. And since she worked at the top genetic lab surrounded by some of the greatest GEI minds in the world, it took a lot to knock her off-kilter. But there was something compelling about this Coder.

In a few great strides, he left B-Watson and crossed the distance between them to stand inches away. His earthy male scent fascinated her—a paradox, considering the near-lethal accusation in his black-brown eyes.

He looked...angry. She retreated a step, then realized her mistake. He eased closer, and she stared up at him.

"Dr. B-Zaika?" He lifted a thick, raven-black eyebrow.

"Yes. How can I help you?"

Did she know this man? She didn't think so. But the intensity of his gaze suggested *he* knew *her*. She peered past his broad shoulders to where Harry hurried to catch up.

"This is Lieutenant York Richmond, Chicago PD," Harry B-Watson said when he reached them.

An invisible capsule of tension crackled around them. Lieutenant Richmond offered her a tight nod. Police didn't frequent genetics centers. What was going on?

Her anxiety escalated with his silent, critical glare. Did she measure up? No, she didn't think so. Different standards. He was of the Coder race—people who descended organically from one generation to the next as far back as the beginning of time. The foolish debate regarding gene manipulation raging between his people and her own GEI race had been going on forever. Still, Kindra got the impression the cosmic heat shield of hostility he emanated arose from far more than basic ideological differences. Somehow, this was…personal for him.

"You're the genetics specialist?"

"Yes." She put on a winning smile, then turned to B-Watson. "Is the Samuel Experiment complete yet?"

He indicated it was not, then trotted off. The clack of his shoes echoed in the cavernous lab. Good or bad, she didn't want her assistant meddling in whatever the police were here for.

She faced the handsome lieutenant. "It's most unusual to have a detective visit Seville. What brings you here?"

"I've been instructed to escort you to the Lakeshore District morgue."

Her stomach flipped before making a hard landing. Not in a million years would she have expected that. "The morgue? Why would I need—"

"Tell me about D-Generation," he cut in.

A prickle of fear skated along her spine. "D-Generation?"

Brianna. She resisted the urge to scream. *Is my baby okay?* Tension darted through her, out of control. When she finally looked him in the eye, he stared at her as if anticipating more information.

"Yes, D," he said.

She drew in a calming breath, forcing composure to overrule her shaken nerves. *Be reasonable.* In an instant, she could display the top-secret details on the overhead instructional computer.

"Perhaps I should check with—"

"I have the required authority," he said.

"Secure ID level?"

"Yes." He sighed impatiently. "Crescent M."

She should ask him for his credentials. Kindra eyed him, hesitant, then shrugged, deciding he'd earned the lightning version at least. "The main difference between C and D-Generations is the Committee narrowed the physical choices—"

"Incredible how you scientists keep doing that." He uttered *scientists* as though it were a filthy occupation.

She ignored his tone. "And they increased the intellectual potential by three standard deviations."

"Oh, Jesus."

"These children are beyond genius level." Kindra smiled, thinking of her own daughter, then reminded herself she'd better find out what this was all about. She could think of only one reason to visit a morgue. "Why are genetics of interest to you, Lieutenant?"

"There's been a D-Generation death."

"An accident?" She struggled to conceal her distress.

"No. Not that we can tell." His gaze homed in on her. "We don't have answers yet. But we need to start with natural causes."

"That's impossible. Why, a D-Generation child would be no more than—"

"Two. The girl would have been three in a few weeks." His jaw tensed, creating a chain reaction of muscles rippling to his dark brow. "A prominent and very distraught family is insisting on an investigation. It's a requirement, regardless. These things aren't supposed to happen."

"No. No, they're not." A rush of relief filled her lungs. Thank God it wasn't *her* little girl. At once, a rain of guilt drowned the thought. Somewhere in the city, another mother had to be inconsolable.

In the past, Kindra may not have reacted so powerfully. Somehow, motherhood had opened a depth of emotion inside her. She'd seen the shift happen with other GEIs when children entered their lives, but she'd never expected to feel it herself.

Kindra felt the blood drain from her face, and her

pulse raced. *Stay professional.* "Computer, the D-Generation design, please." Raising her hand, she directed the officer's attention to the holographic screen at the end of the room. "Take a look, Lieutenant. Ds are expected to have an average life span of one hundred and sixty years."

"Holy sh—"

A ribbon of pride danced through her at his amazement. Genetic engineering had changed the course of history. GEIs were the product of the twenty-first century's California quest for cosmetic perfectionism—the ideal body, complexion, hair, and eyes. Then intellect became a hot commodity. Now, people could purchase it—and even change it—for the right price, including perfect children comprised of features chosen from an enhancement catalog. *Designer babies*, some called them. York was correct—her people simply didn't die. Not until the brain gave out. That was the one thing they couldn't clone. A sister facility of the Seville worked on cloning body parts, and her fellow scientists constantly developed and refined techniques to increase the speed at which they could grow body parts.

On some gut level, Kindra detested the idea her parents had created her as part of a fad for perfection and beauty, though she couldn't blast the benefits of an increased life span with immunity to all known illnesses. It seemed most other people appreciated the advantage of that sort of manipulation, too—even Coders. The days of cancer and disease were behind them, and that was a far more important outcome than simply being pretty.

She lifted a holograph pad from the desk, then plopped it back. Information about germ lines and stem and somatic cells scrolled across the enormous display. She hugged herself, trying to still a sudden sense of unease.

What had caused the child's death? Had she been murdered? Or was there an undetected mistake in the genetics? Would such a mistake be present in all

D-Generation children, or could the error be restricted to the one deceased child? Kindra forced herself not to jump to conclusions while tempering her urge to analyze. Minor tweaks in the genome could produce major changes. This turn of events gave her even more reasons to urge for a delay in the E-Generation release. In her estimation, they were moving too far, too fast. She knew what was at stake. And she knew who they would blame if something went awry—*her*.

An almost overwhelming feeling of powerlessness and guilt came over her. Kindra couldn't help but wonder if she had done something to contribute to the unknown little girl's death. She could only imagine how she'd feel if something happened to her child. She glanced sideways at the lieutenant, pushing the thought aside.

Evidence. That was what she needed. No sense getting worked up without the facts.

Lieutenant Richmond studied the screen, and she observed him. His unruly eyebrows furrowed above intense dark eyes. Short wisps of hair curled past the clean neckline of his blue shirt. She blinked, lacing her fingers together. He, no doubt, had too much hair—an unpleasant trait of Coders, with their unkempt shadow beards. GEIs hadn't been engineered to have facial hair. Only smooth perfection. Even so, she wondered how his hair would feel. Soft? Springy? Coarse? A curious knot tightened in her chest.

Unfolding her arms, she drew her attention to the screen and the data she knew by rote. It was information she'd learned at her father's knee. Robert A-Zaika had always found time to answer her questions, always encouraged her, always had confidence in her. On a heavy sigh, she resolved to keep her emotions in check. This wasn't about her parents.

When the data ceased flickering over the display, Lieutenant Richmond shifted toward her with an unexpected look of…admiration?

"You understand that?"

Kindra gave an abrupt nod. Few people saw what she did as anything special. "I'll need to examine the girl, run tests, and meet with the medical examiner. But I have a petition I'm scheduled to present to the Committee in..." She checked the clock on the table. "Oh my. Ten minutes. I can't leave until I'm finished with that."

York crossed his arms over his chest. "What could be so important? Doesn't it bother you a child has died?"

"Of course it does."

"Then reschedule the meeting."

Kindra hesitated. "It's not that easy."

"It would be if it were *your* child."

Inhaling sharply, she pressed her lips together. "There's nothing I can do for that child now. But my report could influence the quality of life for millions of people in the next generation, so you're welcome to wait here until I'm done, or I can meet you at the morgue."

His jaw firm, he bit out, "I'll wait."

She snatched the computer key for her presentation from the desk. "Suit yourself."

To her irritation, he followed a few steps behind her. At first, she thought he was going to hang out in the outer office, but he stayed with her as she moved into the hall. What was with this guy? She clenched her teeth in annoyance, but then immediately imagined the way her father used to tap her jawline to break her of the habit.

On a long, slow exhale, she tried to focus on the major points of her presentation and ignore Lieutenant Richmond, hoping he'd give up and go away. If she didn't know better, she'd think he considered her a flight risk.

As she navigated the halls to the conference room, a door suddenly opened. A technician darted out, forcing Kindra and York to stop short. Kindra shifted her gaze to the slowly closing door, peeking inside. Lights glowed in a dim blueish hue. She could see the Artificial Wombs lined up in rows. It had been a long while since she'd ventured there. Not since before Brianna was born.

In a flash of memory, she considered the way GEI children were conceived and born. Usually, the mature egg and sperm were retrieved from the prospective parents, combined in the lab, then genetically altered according to the parents' choices selected from a list of attributes dictated by the Committee. Viable unions were implanted into an Artificial Womb to grow and mature until gestation was complete.

Kindra caught the lieutenant's gaze also locked on the room. His face darkened, perhaps because he didn't approve of the birth method. Most Coders didn't. For GEI, it was simply the way it was done, as opposed to the Coder's, who propagated through intercourse.

One thing both groups shared, though, was there were no unwanted children in this day and age. Birth control had moved far beyond accidental pregnancies. All children were wanted, except for the ones the Committee deemed imperfect.

Kindra stopped outside the conference room door. Anxiety squeezed her stomach, and the leaden ball that had been her breakfast moved higher into her chest. Her heart raced. "You can't go in. Wait here."

AVAILABLE NOW

———————

Read on for a sneak peek of *Awakening Touch*.

You met Seth in *Forever at Risk*
Now see him where his legacy on earth began in

AWAKENING FIRE

THE DIVINE TREE GUARDIAN SERIES

LARISSA EMERALD

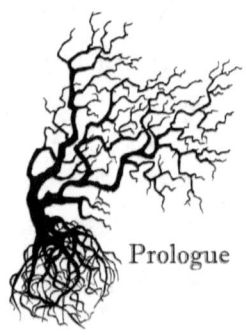

Prologue

Isle of Skye, Scotland
1120 AD

The crusty old man with long ropes of coal-black hair didn't look like an angel, but he had earned the attention of Venn and his eleven brothers. With a flick of the wrist, the angel plucked an enormous boulder into the air and dropped it on the snarling barghest, plastering the demon onto the ground.

"Guid God, that was close." Minutes ago, he'd thought he and his brothers would all be dead as, in force, they'd fought against the barthest that had attacked them from out of nowhere. Then that angel had joined their ranks and outdone them all. With heaving breaths, Venn crouched near the fire pit and thrust his sword into the flames. As the beast's thick, yellow blood sizzled on the metal, Venn's brothers gathered in a loose semicircle: Njorth, Ian, Euler,

Rurik, Aidan, Brandt, Colby, Graham, Dustin, Tristan, Lachlan. All alive. Bruised, bloodied, clothing clawed and shredded. But alive. Thanks be to God.

Seth, as the angel called himself, perched atop the sandstone rock, apparently fishing dirt from under his fingernails. Beneath him, the boulder flattened the malicious barghest facedown into the dirt, limbs and head protruding, far larger than the biggest dog Venn had ever seen. A foul odor of rotten eggs permeated the air as the thing fought mightily against the stone's weight. The barghest scored the earth with four-inch claws, flashed fangs the length of swords, and snarled.

Venn coughed at the stench, then winced as a biting pain seized his rib.

"Finish off the monster," Njorth, the eldest brother, demanded.

"Nay." Seth breathed deeply. His wings expanded and retracted in time with each inhalation. "Io will not die this day. My brother is cast into a net by his own feet." With one hand reaching skyward, he summoned a somewhat smaller boulder at cliff's edge, which he dropped on the barghest's protruding head. "That may silence him for a while."

The rasp in the angel's voice brought to mind wheels catching on rough ground. "'Tis said that each man's future is written before it occurs." Seth passed his perceptive gaze over the brothers. When he came to Venn, his expression darkened, his eyes narrowed. "And 'tis true. Well, partially so. Occasional exceptions have been known to alter one's course. Brothers, you have been chosen."

Venn stood, met the angel's piercing blue stare, and sheathed his sword. A biting wind scurried along the embankment at his back, then shot out over the cliff to meet the riotous waves, enhancing the swirl and shift of the late-morning fog.

The brothers were border guards, protecting their kin

against skirmishes and raiding. Venn had been the last invited to this gathering, most likely due to his fierce disbelief in angels.

Not anymore.

"The two prime virtues ascribed to Highlanders are fidelity and courage. This day thou art offered a great challenge to draw on both of these merits." Seth glanced to the enormous tree several rods from the brothers as he circled his hand upward in a dramatic flourish.

The undercurrent in the air changed, foretelling an approaching storm. The ground shook with an intensity that sent Venn tumbling to the dirt. He rolled sideways to avoid the fire but still fell close enough to it to singe his hair. The pungent burned smell pinched his nose. He staggered to his feet.

As he got his bearings and raised his head, a tremendous sound akin to a ship splitting in half thundered painfully through his ears and chest. The tree rose, uprooted like God himself had reached down and plucked it from the earth. Soil and rocks dropped away, and Venn shifted his stance, muscles tensed, as his fight-or-flight instinct warred within.

Suspended in midair a furlong overhead, the tree began to rotate. Agonizingly slow, at first, then faster and faster, gaining momentum. Clumps of earth flew from the roots as a rain of rock and mud pelted the ground. Within the space of a few breaths, the oak created a whirl of limbs and branches, and leaves peeled away. Venn recoiled, shielding his eyes, as a burst of white light and a deafening boom pummeled them all. He glanced up in time to glimpse the trunk splintering apart, chunks of tree launching skyward and soaring across the land in every direction.

And then it was gone.

The maelstrom was over as quickly as it had begun, and twelve forked sticks dropped at Seth's feet. Venn cursed under his breath and palmed his bearded face. What had they just witnessed?

He sprinted toward Njorth and clasped his elder brother's arm, ready to drag him away from the alleged angel.

Seth shot him a reproachful glare, then knelt to retrieve the sticks. "Peace!" He tossed one to each of the twelve brothers, saving Venn for last.

Venn had not intended to comply with the angel's bidding, but he caught the stick instinctively. As soon as his hand closed around the rough wood, an odd burning sensation spread under his skin, followed by pain slicing through him from neck to groin.

What had the angel done?

A pleased, knowing smile broke across Seth's face as spasms continued twisting in Venn's chest. He groaned, hearing his brothers do the same. He turned to find their heads thrown back, their arms spread wide, all seeming to be experiencing the same horror he was.

The sequence coursed through Venn three agonizing times. When the fit subsided, he gasped airless pants as if he'd raced across several deep furrows.

Seth's smile vanished. "For every honest man bent to the purpose of noble deeds, there are thousands driven by greed, lust, revenge, and power. Hundreds vying for the secrets of youth, the secrets of the universe, the secrets to manipulating time and space. Men whose misplaced allegiance increases evil."

Venn balanced the stick in his palm and tested its weight, curiosity replacing his agony. Oddly heavy, it felt like part of him, an extension of his arm.

"The Divine Tree has splintered and will take root in new domains. Thou hast been given a divining rod to direct you to your tree. As Immortal Guardians, you are to protect that tree and its secrets with your life. But most importantly...do not allow the Dark Realm entry into the tree. And if your tree dies, so shall you. And all of humanity will suffer the consequences for the loss of its knowledge. Go, and be well."

As if that explained everything, Seth disintegrated into shimmering particles that faded to nothing.

"Wait," Venn called. Immortal Guardians? Tales of Odin and Yggdrasill and the Christian uprising vied in a mist of confusion.

Why would Venn and his brothers be called to guard anything? Seth must be mad.

Venn tossed the divining rod aside. "Firewood," he scoffed.

When he looked up, he met his brothers' disapproving stares as they gathered their belongings. Njorth prodded his injured thigh, where an ugly gash oozed red. He grimaced, raised and lowered his leg. Then the wound dried up and closed.

His eyes widened. "Look at that. Healed." He turned to his brothers, each of them looking in turn to see the cut now gone. He gave a small chuckle. "Oh, but it aches like hell."

"Stop complaining," their brother Ian grumbled.

Njorth gave Venn a hearty clap on the shoulder, a wallop meant to suffice for a long time. "This ain't half-bad."

They were *immortal?* No, it wasn't possible.

Part of him wanted to ignore Seth's directives as nonsense and head home, but he stole another glance at Njorth's healed thigh. He eyed his other brothers, packed and ready, each fisting their shares of the tree. He swallowed, pulling a sheepskin pouch over his shoulder as his heartbeat escalated with indecision, then slowed in resignation.

Ah, hell, brothers fought side by side. He trod toward the fire pit to retrieve his divining rod from where he'd thrown it. As he fisted the wood, a prickling force pulsed up into his arm and shoulder, the rod seeming to yank him to the east. He shook off the feeling, his attention was forced back to the barghest, whose menacing paws thrashed from beneath the boulders, announcing that its wild nature had revived.

"I can't stand that beast," Euler declared. He raised his sword, stepping closer to Io. "Let's take his head and be done with him while we can."

"No." Seth's booming voice crashed over them like a rolling wave.

"Hope he stays under there 'til he rots," Njorth grumbled.

Venn backed cautiously away, a hand on his sword hilt, allowing a wide berth for the beast's vicious claws. "Let's go. I suggest we figure out the game rules somewhere else. Before we hav'ta yield more of our blood."

1

Present Day

At the subterranean entrance to the Divine Tree sanctuary, Venn Hearst halted and raised his eyes to the etchings of a wolf and hawk emblazoned in the aged wood above the door, a nod to his alternate forms. Venn extended his tattooed wrist, positioning the elaborately inked tree, and the pulsing artery beneath it, below a glistening twisted root for the anointing ritual. An amber-colored drop of sap spilled over the image, then pooled and bubbled before it was absorbed into his skin, sending a sharp zing to each of his neurons before settling within the larger matching tat on his back.

The language of the universe rustled through the air. The Secrets men died to know, Guardians swore to protect, and the Dark Realms were determined to steal or destroy were housed within this sacred place.

His Divine Tree was one of the original dozen hidden around the globe. There were eleven left after the Divine Tree Guardians had lost his brother Tristan along with the Divine Tree in Germany in the mid-nineteen hundreds. The tree's demise had caused the earth to shift on its axis ever so slightly, bringing them one step closer to Armageddon with an escalation of malevolent forces. Evil had blossomed with Hitler taking millions of lives before balance could be restored. It had been an uphill battle ever since.

Venn opened and closed his fist, considering the tattoo on his wrist. Not even one more tree could be lost.

"Benison," the oak whispered.

"Blessings," Venn returned. "My strength and loyalty are yours."

With his vow, the door to the tree creaked opened, and he strode through the massive entry. He looked around the comfortable aboveground chambers and kept walking. Keeping watch wasn't his intention this night. No, he sought the tombs within the root structure below and hoped the tree would communicate to him if something out of the ordinary was happening.

He grabbed a nearby flashlight from the alcove next to the door, flipped it on, and started along the narrow tunneled path, down a staircase that had been fashioned by twisted knots of wood and roots fused together over centuries. It wound deep into the layers of knowledge, to the catacomb of interconnected scripts, like a true, living computer.

Once in the belly, he ran a hand over an electrical switch. Battery powered lights illuminate the cave-like room in a pale glow. Venn glanced about and drew an awed breath. *Holy shit. The place had grown.*

With careful steps, he moved from the tunnel into a cavern, where rough splinters jutted out of smooth swirls in the timber's pattern, creating a golden wooden cave. He used to come down here often in the beginning, during the early years of loneliness, always expecting to discover something exceptional. Which he usually did.

He'd learned that if he pricked himself on this special wood, a series of images would fire though his brain, teaching him something new, its lessons sharper and more thorough than those of any history or science channel on TV.

Centuries ago, he'd stumbled on this cavern and its amazing phenomenon quite by accident. The power the tree gave him had become an obsession, the data exchange an addiction. He knew better than to come back again after that. But this time he had no choice, his duty demanded he use every means available to him. He was well aware of the risks and didn't intend to overstep his limits.

Something was off-kilter in the universe, and he needed to know why. The odd weather pattern—winter when it should be spring—was an ominous sign, Venn knew, even if humans simply took it as a fluke of nature. Just as humans showed symptoms of illness, so too did the machinations of the universe. And a shift between good and evil often triggered such nasty weather patterns.

He needed to be on high alert. "Custos," he spoke quietly to the ancient tree. "Do you know what's going on?"

There was no answer.

Taking a seat in a worn cradle of wood, he felt the need to connect with the Divine Tree…and to his brothers. He squeezed the back of his neck. Perhaps that's what the problem was. Not outside at all, but within him.

He felt as isolated from everything as this tree was. What was it like to house all humanity but not feel humanity?

The groan and creak of the tree, as if it were caught by a strong gust of wind, caused Venn to lift his head. Seth stood framed in the tunnel doorway. "I didn't think you'd be down here," the angel said, walking into the chamber.

Now Venn *knew* there was trouble brewing. The angel rarely dropped in just to say hello. "What's happenin'?" Venn asked in way of greeting.

Seth shrugged, his wings lifting and falling with the movement. "I'm not sure. But you must feel it also if you're down here."

"Indeed. Have a seat," Venn motioned to another curve of wood.

Seth sat and crossed his legs, resting his back and folded wings against the smooth inner walls of the tree. "I dunno. On one hand the off weather pattern seems like a trivial thing, but coupled with all the unrest in the world—with ISIS beheading people in the Middle East and people protesting over police in the US—I think we need to pay close attention."

"I agree. The planet is digressing into a state of anarchy and I'd bet my right arm that the Dark Realm is behind it all," Venn proclaimed.

"No doubt."

"I think you'd better hang around," Venn suggested.

"Fine. You got a room to spare?" Seth asked, firing a glance from beneath heavy eyelids without lifting his head.

"No."

Seth shrugged. "Then I can't help you."

Venn chuckled, knowing full well he'd just gained a house guest. "It's hard to think back to when this guardianship began." He rested his head back and closed his eyes, trying to see that far into the past. "You know you could have given us a little more information when you set us on this task."

"What for? You figured it out."

"Huh. It took me forever to learn to control my shifting. The hawk being able to manipulate time and space, and the wolf's incredible strength. Shit, I was a mess in those days."

"You're still a mess," Seth said with exaggerated distain.

Venn straightened. "Hey, I didn't ask for this gig. You can head back up anytime."

Emma sympathized with anyone who had to make transatlantic flights on a regular basis. The trip from Paris to Atlanta's Hartsfield-Jackson airport had left her weary as a rag doll. Two hours later, she was still stifling yawns as she surveyed the snow-covered park where her mélange-metal statue would reside.

"I'm sorry. I shouldn't have made you stop here on the way from the airport. You must be exhausted." Grams tugged the zipper of her trendy black leather jacket higher before passing the leash attached to her little, aging Yorkshire terrier, Izzy, from one hand to the other. The pup scooted around her legs. "It was thoughtless of me. I'm just so excited."

Emma shrugged. "I'm fine," she assured her grandmother, then twisted to face the trunk of the enormous tree they stood beneath when the next yawn came. A whisper of energy coiled around her, heat seeming to seep out of the bark itself. She pursed her mouth and clasped her arms around her rib cage. As if the move offered any protection. Fatigue always made her paranoid. She even sometimes saw visions, though she didn't like to admit it, even to herself.

She sighed. No use in worrying about something she couldn't control, and she'd long since learned she wasn't in the driver's seat where her visions were concerned. Instead, she engaged in her most prevalent form of evasion, her art.

Nothing wrong with burying problems in a little work.

She studied the space again. Which metals would capture the hues of oyster shells in the sky? What subject would best fit the colors? Emma jotted down some mental notes for her next project. She watched the changing colors of dusk descend on the park as clouds loomed, back-lit in an eerie coppery shimmer. The diffused light made the snow appear almost warm, the rocks somehow spongy, and the trees… They were mystical.

Her apprehension escalated as the walkway in front of her blurred. Her knees grew weak.

No. Not this time.

She sucked in a deep breath and tensed, resisting. But she knew with sickening certainty that the vision was coming. There was no controlling it…

An arrow shaft protruded from her chest, and air wheezed through her stagnant lungs. In the wake of the brutal, radiating pain, time slowed. Her heart stopped.

Oh God.

An image of a huge gray wolf materialized, howling a cry of grief alongside her lifeless body, and it lingered, dimming slowly to a sepia shadow. Had she…died here?

Emma blinked, disoriented, as the brief manifestation faded, reality setting back in. Exhaling hard, she shifted her feet, peering down at her strappy, crystal-embellished, leopard-print sandals and seeking solid ground. Izzy licked at her toes where they peeked from her shoes, as if trying to console her as best he could.

Her gaze swept up her own body, and she settled shaky fingers over her beating heart. No blood. No arrow. Definitely alive.

Still, the suffocating sensation of a collapsed lung remained, causing her stomach to churn. How she even knew what one felt like alarmed her.

Stop thinking about it.

With determined strength, Emma overcame the pervasive mental intrusion, forcing her attention back to the grossly neglected Georgia park where she stood trembling, to the place her sculpture would call home.

She'd had these dreams and visions her whole life, and when she'd researched the phenomenon, she'd discovered they were each giving her a glimpse of one of her past lives. If one believed in that sort of thing. Which she did. But knowing that didn't make it any less disturbing.

Emma's breath swirled in a misty cloud as she focused on her surroundings. Cold, damp air patted her cheeks. The massive oak before her released a sad moan. Or was that just her active imagination at work? Whatever it was triggered a familiar warmth that spread into her limbs, and reminded her she possessed...talents beyond her visions. Heat radiated through her right arm, and she glanced down, opening her blazing hot fist to discover she'd inadvertently melted her grandmother's butterfly key fob beyond recognition.

Some *talents*. More like she'd been cursed.

With an unsteady sigh, she pushed her hair away from her face. Geez, her life hadn't changed one iota. Since she was a toddler, she'd been molding metal with her bare hands as if it were clay, both intentionally and accidentally. It was the latter that caused her grief. The episode with a neighborhood boy and his squished red Hot Wheels car came to mind. It always did. Her dad had been so angry with her.

"Are you okay?"

Her grandmother's question snapped her back to the present. Would Grams know if she lied? She'd discovered when she'd moved to New York that the visions and dreams had lessened with the distance. She'd run all the way to Paris to avoid them. And they must have let go, too, because she hadn't thought of them for a long, long while.

"Sure. But I can't say the same for this." She dangled the key chain in the air.

Her grandmother gave a chuckle. "I should have nicknamed you Hot Hands."

Emma managed to summon a smile, but it faltered as her gaze shifted back to that tree. Its spindly canopy of branches seemed to reach out. The hair on her arms prickled. Something in the fractures of time yanked free and another ripple of unease washed over her.

Good and evil used this place as a playground. At the moment, evil acted the bully. She felt a bizarre tug-of-war for dominance, the power of it making her sway.

Leave. Me. Alone.

This evening's vision was beyond vivid—a seven-point-five on the Richter scale, and it wasn't passing as it normally did. She flailed her arms, trying to shake off her frustration. She usually had an easier time coming out of it. An erratic pulse thumped in her neck, bringing her circulation back. Her temples ached with the awakening.

She shook her head. *Ignore. Regroup. Move on.*

Thank goodness her grandmother, who tarried a few steps behind, wouldn't know the depth of Emma's latest episode, since time distorted or elongated only within her mind. What she needed was an anchor, physically and mentally. There was no way she'd allow her father to be right about her differences making her crazy. She didn't have a psychotic disorder as he'd suggested when she was young. No, she would control the lapse, but, darn, this bout threatened her common sense. She'd never seen herself die before.

Besides, wasn't that supposed to kill you or something?

Or was that just in dreams, not visions? She gave a mental shrug, figuring it didn't matter because she had both.

Focus. She was here on a job. The park.

It was spring in Tyler, Georgia, yet the late-season snow masked the evidence. Weeds and yellow wildflowers nudged aside a layer of snow, and fresh green growth attempted to unfurl on branches. The square must have been lovely at one time, especially when everything began to bloom, but not now. A battered, rotten wood bench lay on the ground sideways, collapsed. The sidewalk that wound through the center of the park resembled a war zone, with chunks of concrete broken and upended. The branches of the old oak swept the earth. Clearly ignored for many, many years, the mammoth tree looked as if it had never been pruned or shaped.

The untamed tree was so out-of-character for prim-and-proper Georgia. Just like her. Her dad had always proclaimed that her overactive imagination would lead to trouble. If he only knew the whole truth.

A hand slid across Emma's back and bony fingers grasped her shoulder. She almost jumped out of her grandmother's hug.

"Just think, a Grant getting the honor of creating a statue for the old town square. I can hardly believe it." Grams heaved one of her exaggerated, bursting-with-pride sighs, the way she did when the family dinner table was landscaped to perfection.

"You drive a hard bargain, Grams. The committee couldn't say no." And neither could Emma. Her grandmother had requested a sculpture of a confederate soldier on a rearing horse. Not very original, but Emma obliged, thankful for both the much-needed income and the chance to build her portfolio. She gradually relaxed into the woman's solid embrace, somewhat grounded again.

She touched her head to her grandmother's salon-teased auburn one, in the same let's-stick-together way she'd done since she was six, when she'd spent every summer vacation here after her family had moved to New York.

"Thanks for your help," Emma said. Nothing like getting paid to visit her favorite relative. Since the city had commissioned her sculpture for the park renovation project, she'd be hanging out for the next few weeks to supervise its placement and participate in the dedication ceremony.

Grams nodded. "Anytime. Paris is too darn far away, if you ask me." She picked Izzy up and tucked him beneath her arm.

Actually, the greater distance meant fewer visions, so it wasn't even far enough. Emma wasn't sure why, but they seemed to be worse, more frequent, when she returned to her Georgia birthplace. Bonus points for Paris.

"We talk and Skype all the time," Emma pointed out.

"That's not the same as seeing your smiling face." Her grandmother slid a hand down Emma's arm and back up over her shoulder. "Look at you. You're shivering."

Ominous gray clouds were moving in, and the sky was growing darker. Emma felt more than saw the clump of wet red clay that oozed into her Sam Edelman sandals. She tamped her foot against a rock to clear it. "What an awful spring. Can't believe it snowed on Easter."

"Yes. The pecan blooms froze. The crop'll be ruined." A smile lit Grams's eyes, and she tsked, seeming to dismiss the unfortunate prediction that might steal her pocket money. "But give it a few days. It'll warm up."

"I'll hold you to that."

Tree branches whipped one way, then the other, generating an eerie whistling. Emma shuddered, then tugged the neckline of her suddenly constricting turtleneck sweater as she turned to explore a staked-out plot of ground. "It looks like this is where they plan to put the statue."

Her gaze swept along the snow-patched ground, up the broken walkway, to the side of the park where fluorescent-orange construction fencing sectioned off individual trees, marking them for protection. Landscaping equipment near the road formed a neat line, ready to be put to use.

A tiny ping caught in her gut, and her internal compass gravitated to the old oak standing center stage. Its trunk stretched out to the size of a small house, as if several trees had grown together. She frowned as intense golden eyes seemed to peer at her from the grained bark. A figment of her imagination? With her history, it had to be.

When the eyes vanished, she angled her head, unable to shake the weird drag on her heart. As if she should know something important, yet couldn't bring it forth. The feeling didn't seem like a remnant of her vision but felt like it originated from an entirely different source. More like an unfathomable power or presence. She scanned the park and rubbed her chilled arms, but she didn't see a single soul.

Io slipped behind the downed bulldozer bucket, in predator mode, his eyes fixed on his target: Emma Grant. The machine inched to the side as his back jammed against a metal support. In his eagerness, he hadn't sufficiently controlled his brute strength. He grumbled at the oversight but kept tuned to the young woman. While in human form, as he was now, his senses were faulty. It was a weak form, practically useless, with few special powers.

He'd known the moment Emma Grant had set foot on Georgia soil.

Not such a difficult task, really. He'd been expecting her.

Now, he was curious about the reason she'd stopped at the park on her way from the airport. Was the Divine Tree's power already blooming in Emma? Had the old tree spoken to her?

He'd met her quite by accident years ago when she was a little girl of five. They were in an ice cream shop and he'd accidently dropped a handful of coins on the floor—as fine motor skills was another issue he had with the human form. But it turned into a fortunate event for him, really, for Emma gathered the coins up off the floor. And to her great embarrassment, when she handed them back to him the lot was fused together in a solid clump of metal.

He knew then and there that she was gifted. And he made it his business to discover why. Eavesdropping in on her dreams at night gave him the connection to her past. Even over the years after she moved from Tyler, he managed to keep track of her. He was damned proud of himself for discovering the reason behind her metal-altering ability.

Well, it wasn't precisely *his* discovery, but he would take credit for it nonetheless.

When he'd killed Emma in her past life and she'd lain on the grassy ground with his arrow jutting out of her chest, her blood had seeped into this magical oak's roots. Who knew such a simple act would create the catalyst to destroy a Divine Tree? He certainly hadn't. Not until the High Counsel of Devils had recently congratulated him for it, that is. And he wasn't disappointed.

That arrow, her blood, and her reincarnation had caused a shift, something even he couldn't grasp the implications of. It had taken him shitloads of long, painful, boring hours of watching before he discovered how he could use her newborn alchemist powers to his advantage. He deserved this boon, and the recognition from the counsel. He'd show his brother, Seth, that he was equally as favored by his superiors.

Now if only he could overcome the free will part of the equation. He couldn't force her into using her alchemist powers on the metal as he wanted her to. At least not physically.

But there were other ways to get the results he desired.

With a mental shake, he glared at Emma.

Did she realize the connection she shared with the tree? If so, he'd have to move much quicker than he'd thought. No, no, he wouldn't allow things to get out of hand. He swiped a restless hand along his jaw.

He tried to quiet the nervous energy that continually tugged him in conflicting directions. One moment he was certain of his mission's success, the next of its failure. His gaze darted from Emma to Mrs. Busybody, listening intently. He plunged his hands into his pockets, withdrew them, then clasped them behind him.

The best he could determine, Emma was simply cold, not agitated or suspicious.

And Mrs. Grant took credit for arranging the commission of the statue her granddaughter had arrived to install.

Yes, it was better that Emma thought her grandmother was the instigator. Better she not discover the significance of the invitation to the installation ceremony. At least not until the ruination of the tree was complete or Emma and the Guardian were dead. Either outcome would give him great pleasure.

After all, he'd discovered firsthand that the best way to make someone suffer was to destroy the one thing that someone most loved. Yes, revenge would be his. About time.

Seth, Mr. Goodie-Goodie, would soon have his world turned upside down. And Venn and the Divine Tree along with him. He could barely contain his excitement. Three for the price of one. Brilliant.

Excited and restless, Io tugged on his shirt sleeve, then sought focus by touching the picture of a burned tree he kept tucked in his pocket. It represented his brother's failure. His channeled hatred grew and his smokescreen, the shield he'd put in place so the tree wouldn't detect his presence, disintegrated. Damn.

The stupid dog in the old ladies arms barked and growled.

A deep moan resounded within the catacomb. *Custos?* Venn straightened from his relaxed position. Immediately, his attention shot upward—above him, outside—and he stood.

What *was* that?

An irresistible tug made him palm his chest. He proceeded through the cavern entrance, back up the knotted stairs and angled tunnel, the pull intensifying with each step. If he were human, he'd be wondering if he were having a heart attack.

He hadn't felt this collision of energy in two centuries.

Inside the sprawling tree, he climbed rough-hewn stairs to the watch room at ground level. He ignored the enormous circular space and its new modular furnishings as he fixed his attention on the highly polished wooden wall, where the force ran strongest. The bark itself had sight, a transparency by which he could see through the layers of wood to the world beyond, at will. He looked out, as he had done so many thousands of times in the past.

Outside, two females engaged in conversation. He immediately recognized Claire Grant. The old lady had been bragging everywhere she went about how her granddaughter, Emma, had designed a sculpture for Tyler's historic town square and oldest park.

Venn's park, not the town's.

But he'd lost that battle a long time ago, and until recently, he had managed to direct the city officials' attentions elsewhere. Damn their renewed interest. The tree had been marked for preservation purposes, which was a good thing, yet it also attracted unwanted attention. There were others who had an inclination of the riches the tree held, not in monetary value but in what they could do with the knowledge contained within.

The presumed granddaughter turned.

Venn advanced to the barrier, curious. He wanted to be closer to her, wanted nothing between them, not this tree, not this space. With his extraordinary sight and hearing, he could make her out perfectly, but it wasn't enough. There was something about her...yet he couldn't fathom why he'd be drawn Claire Grant's granddaughter. How odd.

With a sweeping glance, the young woman arched her brows and strolled toward the tree. She seemed to stare right at him. Thick auburn hair draped over her shoulders, and she tilted her head, his equilibrium shattering. A roar took up residence inside his skull. Thunder vibrated through his chest, and explosive desire made him hard and ready.

His breath hitched. His inner beasts stirred without the customary summons, fighting each other, wolf and hawk vying for a glimpse of her.

She inched forward.

Yes, move closer.

She spoke, and he vaguely caught her whispered French phrase. *"Coeur de mon coeur."*

Heart of my heart.

He swallowed, hard.

She placed a delicate palm on the trunk, and Venn growled as a surge of energy—her very essence—flowed into the tree, filled him as much as earthy air filled his lungs.

"I...feel something," Emma said with opened-mouth awe. "The oak has been here for hundreds of years."

When recognition hit Venn, it was with the force of an 18-wheeler rear-ending a car waiting at a traffic light. Every muscle in his body tensed as he saw flashes of her in a past life, of their limbs entwined, of her lips warm on his, of her vibrant laugh...of her dying.

Could it truly be Amelia? Had she returned to him in this woman, this Emma Grant?

Venn closed his eyes and summoned energy in all its manifested forms—heat, light, sound, magnetism, gravity, and all of life's functions—reaching out to her, touching deep into her soul to test the theory. Her initial response was a lazy yawn, but then her mystical imprint danced, the spirit unique to her, proclaimed, *Yes!*

She. Was. His.

A heaviness slammed against his chest, followed by whiplash, pain, confusion. He'd been robbed of time, his woman, his love.

Ah, Amelia. Brought back to him after so long.

A spark flared in his chest, and his pulse sped up. Unwilling to move lest this sudden feel-good moment disappeared, he held his breath.

She glanced over her shoulder at her grandmother. "I have the strangest feeling of déjà vu."

Overwhelmed, he wished he could vault through the barrier and take her in his arms. Instead, he braced both hands on thick chair arms as he slowly lowered himself into the seat, not taking his eyes off the woman with fiery hair and golden skin. Every fiber in his body stretched out to embrace her. She was his.

They'd been lovers in 1809. Companions. Promised journey mates. A favor from God.

His throat tightened at the memory, and he tried to drink in the air. She was the one woman gifted with the powers to complement his. He hadn't known until too late how much he needed to share his life with someone. And his enemy had murdered her.

She must be the reason the tree summoned him.

He narrowed his eyes, scrutinizing the grounds for yet another assassin. But the only ones there were the Grants.

Uncertain what to expect, he watched, fisting his hand with a vow.

This time he would protect her. This time he would fulfill the promise of a lifetime mate. This time she would be his. Forever.

Emma's brow furrowed as her hand swept along the bark of the tree. *His* tree. "Did I come here as a girl?" she asked. "I seem to know this place."

"I don't think so, child. Your father didn't wander much south of the ravine. Claimed he got bad vibes here. Always afraid, that boy. Not enough faith. Of course, there were all kinds of stories bantered about back then. Some about a man being killed out here, tales about witches and ghosts, you name it. The place became run-down. But with the city rejuvenation and cleanup, well… As you can see, things are different now."

Indeed, things had changed, Venn mused. His mansion lay south of the park, far enough away so as to not attract visitors. A strategic plan he'd sanctioned to assure his privacy. Back in the day, he'd met with wealthy plantation owners and connected politicians on his own terms. Otherwise, he'd avoided them. As time passed and with the never-ending urbanization, he didn't care for the coziness.

When Emma pulled her hand away from the bark, it was like part of him flickered, then snuffed out. He got a mild case of shakes, and his temperature plummeted.

"It's getting late, you must be tired," Mrs. Grant said.

"Nah. I'm a night person, remember? How about if we stop by Aunt Fay's Coffee Shop on the way home? I've been dreaming about one of her famous cinnamon buns all the way here."

"Okay. You drive." She hitched the small dog she held higher under her arm.

They were leaving. With a leap, Venn stood, banging his knee on the side table. He winced and beat back a wave of anxiety. He'd been given a second chance and he'd be damned if he'd let her out of his sight this time. At least, not for long.

Keenly aware that she wouldn't know him in this life, he needed to initiate a meeting. This minute. However, walking up out of nowhere in a shabby park might scare her.

He wished they could simply pick up where they'd left off.

He envisioned her smiling at him with recognition and running into his opened arms.

But as she got closer to the car and farther from him, the vision scattered.

Aunt Fay's. That was it.

He could use a jolt of caffeine.

AWAKENING FIRE is available now!

ACKNOWLEDGMENTS

Many thanks to my fabulous team of professionals:

Cover design: Dreams2media
Interior formatting: Author E.M.S.
Editor: Danielle Poiesz
Editor and proofreader: Cynthia Shepp

About the Author

Larissa Emerald has always had a powerful creative streak whether it's altering sewing patterns, or the need to make some minor change in recipes, or frequently rearranging her home furnishings, she relishes those little walks on the wild side to offset her otherwise quite ordinary life. Her eclectic taste in books cover numerous genres, and she writes sexy contemporary romance, paranormal romance, and futuristic romantic thrillers. But no matter the genre or time period, she likes strong women in dire situations who find the one man who will adore her beyond reason and give up everything for true love.

Larissa is happy to connect with her readers. Stop by and say hello at her website, Facebook, Twitter, or send her an email: larissaemerald@gmail.com.